Lila

BY ROSE ROSS

LILA is a work of fiction. Names, characters, and incidents are products of the author's imagination or are used fictitiously. Any resemblance to actual events, locales or persons living or dead is entirely coincidental.

Print ISBN: 978-0-578-60960-7

Library of Congress
Control Number:2019916898

Cover Photo by Courtney Gilbert
of Peter Lorber Photo Labs

Jacket and Cover design by Andrea Wolga

Published by EDDYPOND

Author's Note

I have learned since becoming a writer that there is a fine line between truth and fiction. This story is both, and one that has been with me for a long time. Growing up is at best complex; growing up as children of Holocaust survivors is even more so. Some second generation children were able to escape the shadow of their parents' suffering, for others their parents' experiences led them unknowingly into an early maturity.

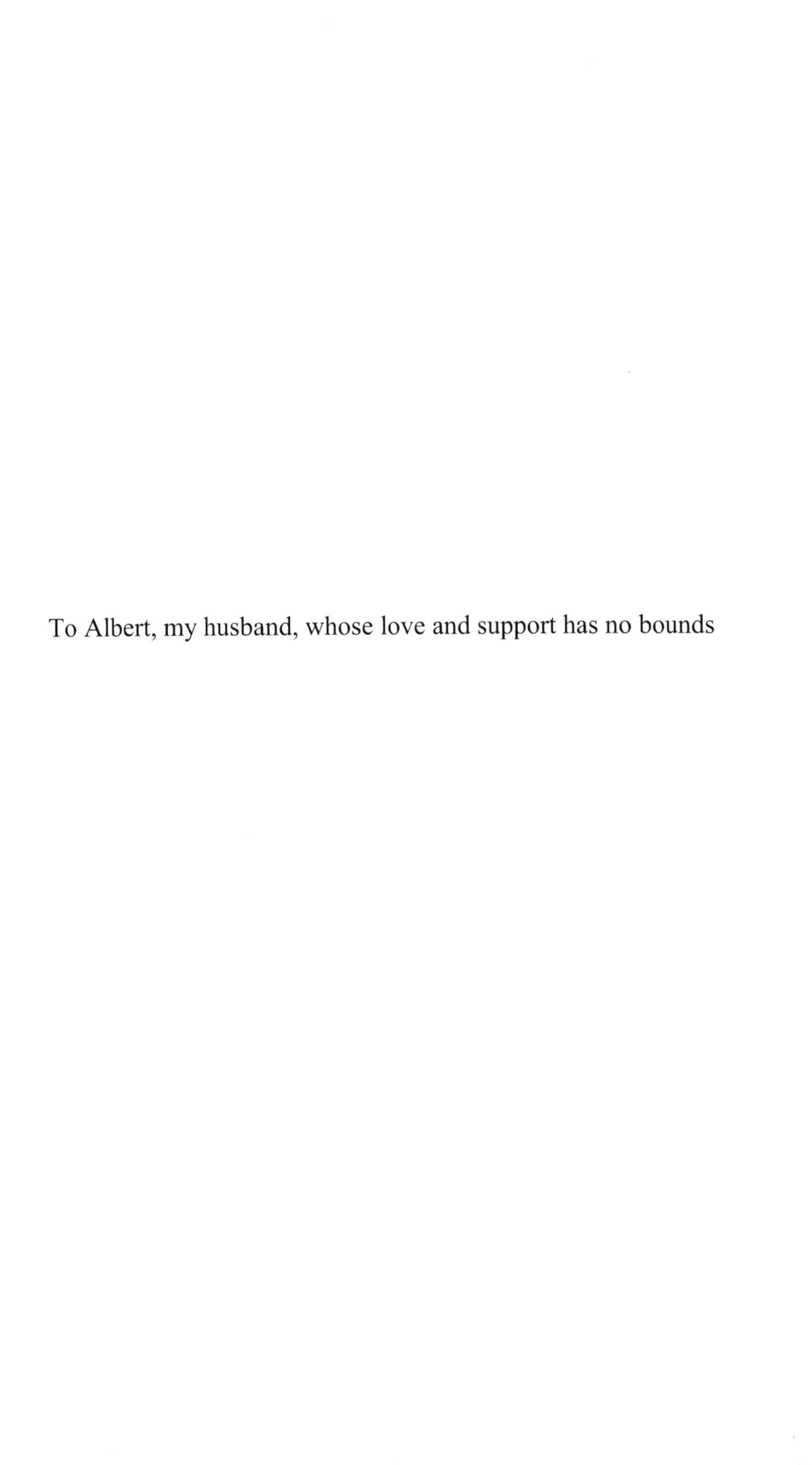

To Albert, my husband, whose love and support has no bounds

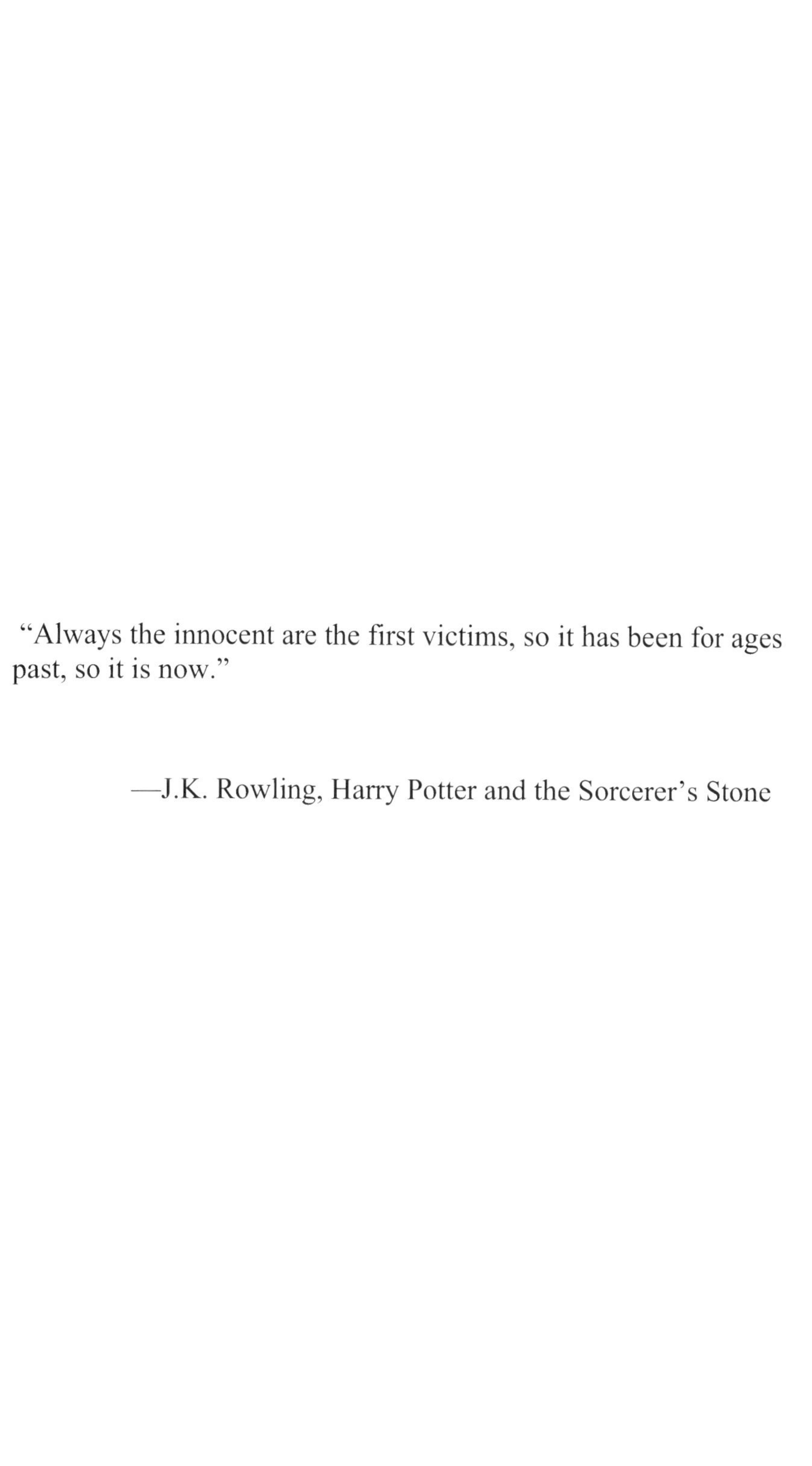

"Always the innocent are the first victims, so it has been for ages past, so it is now."

—J.K. Rowling, *Harry Potter and the Sorcerer's Stone*

Prologue

Sarah – 1980

I shouldn't be here. Too many negative thoughts are running through my head. Who knows, maybe I have some of that "Bad Seed" in me like I always accused Lila of having. It's possible; after all, our parents were Holocaust survivors. Lila and I were born on the same day, same year, and we were the first born in the same Displaced Persons Camp in Germany. Perhaps all the horrors that our parents went through seeped into our souls and made us who we are. I know I'm being my overly dramatic self, but at the time our births were thought to be a miracle. Everyone in the camps believed our lives would be intertwined like silk ribbons on a Maypole, that we were meant to be sisters. Instead, our relationship was always one of competition, envy, manipulation, and, sometimes, rage.

For as long as I can remember I hated Lila Rosen and struggled to keep her out of my life, but not this way. Not at her funeral, on her 34th birthday. And to make it worse, the fourteenth of April, the day of our birthdays, will always and forever also be the day of her death.

Standing behind a tree, I see my parents and the small group of mourners I have known and grown up with since the fall of 1949, when we came from Germany and settled on Westchester Avenue in the South Bronx in New York City. Minnie, Selma, and neighbors from our building, kids from school, including Roxy, even Tommy, and BoBo. Tommy is as handsome as ever; BoBo is pregnant with their third child. Motherhood has not made her any less tough looking. She still scares the hell out of me. I'm in disbelief but not surprised at the sorrow and shock on all their faces. To them, Lila was the beautiful angel with blue eyes that shone like glass and blonde hair as smooth as silk. No one here believed the stories, the rumors that were repeated over the years, except for Michael and me. We knew that they were more than possible because we were victims of Lila's vengeance. I turn around, hoping to see him. He promised to take the first flight out of Paris, where he now lives. *Where is he?* I know I'm sounding incredibly selfish, but Michael can always reach into the better part of me. In his magical way, only he can make me deal with my lack of compassion for Lila. I just wish he were here now.

Suddenly I hear cries, moaning. There is a commotion. I run to Mom and Dad. We watch in horror as Max Rosen jumps out of his seat, thrusting his body onto the ground at the foot of Lila's grave. His hands are clawing at the dirt, trying to grasp the casket as it is being lowered. Lila's name escapes from his throat and echoes hauntingly as lightning sweeps across the sky. The Rabbi pulls Max away. Someone shouts out STOP! We all turn to see Fritzy stoically stand up and slowly raise her veil. Without shame, for all to see and hear, she spits at Max as his body crumbles to the ground.

"Go with your whore of a daughter. May you both burn in hell!"

I have the sensation that something has broken within me. Can I actually be experiencing sympathy? Pity? But for who, Max? Fritzy? Lila? Tears fall down my cheeks. I feel so utterly helpless. Then a hand takes mine. It's Michael. As I gaze into his eyes, the memories of our friendship, my battle to be free of Lila, my guilt, all flash through my mind.

Introduction

1952 - 1957

Friday Night Games

The second Friday of every month, the Lanins and the Rosens had card night. Max, Fritzy, and Lila Rosen went to the Lanins' apartment for a meal of deli, gossip, Kaluki, and poker. On the fourth Friday of every month, the Lanins went to the Rosens'. Before each of those Friday nights, I asked my Mom the same question, "Mom, why, do we have to see them all the time? You don't like Fritzy, she doesn't like you, and I hate Lila!"

One card night when I was nine, Mom got tired of my asking. She told me to sit down and gave me *the talk*: "Sarah, enough with the whining. And I do not want to hear any more about this hate business. Trust me. I have had enough of that for a lifetime. Besides, I did not survive a war to raise you to hate. The Rosens, for better or worse, are the closest thing we have to a family. AND it is what it is! Now, stop being a baby."

"But, Mom, you never listen to me," I cried out.

"Sarah, sit!" commanded Mom.

I wanted to continue arguing with her, but I knew she meant business. I sat down, crossed my elbows, sucked in my cheeks, and waited for whatever lesson was to come next.

"Now, I am going to tell you a story and I want you should listen carefully and then maybe you will understand, all right?"

I made a face, squeezed my lips tight and gave in.

"Sarah, what makes the Rosens and the Lanins family is you and Lila."

Not again, I thought. I had heard this story over and over. Lila and I being born on the same day and because of that we were meant to be like "sisters." Well, it didn't happen like that and never would. I knew I was going to be bored listening to this.

"Sarah, if you do not get that expression off your face, trust me, you will be sorry," said Mom, seriously.

"Most of us women who survived the concentration camps never thought that our bodies would be able to be healthy again, let alone be strong enough to bear a child. So when Fritzy and I became pregnant at the same time, what can I tell you, it was the miracle of all miracles. But, as happy as we were, we were also afraid. So many nights I did not sleep because all I could think about was, what if God was testing us again? Could he be that cruel? Was this a joke he was playing? Would I lose this baby? Would it be deformed? Would it be stillborn? Oh, the terrible things that went through my head. Fritzy and I never talked about our fears because we thought they could bring us bad luck.

"I prayed every minute of every day and night that you would be born with all your fingers, toes, feet, arms, that your body would not be twisted or bent. In the camps, the doctors stuck many needles into us. They made us swallow big pills, little pills. They would force bad-smelling liquids down our throats and they would watch us as if we were animals in a cage. Then, of course, there were the beatings. The guards took so much pleasure in beating us, whipping us. All the time, they laughed and laughed, especially when they used our stomachs as a punching bag one blow after another until we collapsed. This was to make sure that we could never bring another Jew into the world.

"Then, the two of you were born on the same day, three hours apart. Oh, how beautiful the both of you were, perfect, with everything in place. So from that day on our families were connected—forever. Everyone thought it was *beshart*. We believed that the two of you would grow up like sisters."

Up to that day, Mom had never talked about what the doctors did to her or, for that matter, anything about her life in the camps. I got up from the chair and literally threw myself at her, hugging her as hard as I could. In my head, I was cursing all of the doctors, all of the Nazis who had hurt her, wishing they had all died painful and horrible, disgusting deaths. Mom put my head on her lap and caressed my hair. She went on.

"The war changed all of us, Sarah. Who knows, maybe Fritzy did not always have a heart made of stone, but she does now. This is what Lila has to live with. Thank God Max has enough love for Lila to make up for what Fritzy cannot give. So maybe once in a while it would not hurt you to be a little kinder to Lila, OK? Now, please, darling, put a smile on your face and help me finish up. They will be here any minute."

I gave Mom the smile that she needed to see. I even told her I was sorry for being the way I was. That I would try to be nicer to Lila. I realized I could never tell her about the true Lila; it would have made her too sad. I put out the candies, helped Mom with the table, and waited for them to arrive.

As always, Fritzy walked in first with the same sour expression on her face. Behind her were Max and Lila, arm in arm, laughing out loud and sharing a joke, carrying on like they were boyfriend and girlfriend. When they acted like this it gave me the creeps. As always, Lila rushed up to Mom and showered her with kisses and hugs. Fritzy watched and cringed at the affection Lila gave to Mom.

After supper and cleanup, our parents were ready to start their card game. And like every second Friday and fourth Friday of the month, Lila turned to me and gave me one of her sly smiles, the one that only I ever saw. She grabbed my hand and, like a good girl, I followed her into my parents' bedroom and wondered what game she had in store for us that night.

The games started when we were six. They were innocent. We played with dolls, colored in coloring books. When we were seven, we played dress-up with my mom's shoes, jewelry, and dresses. We never did this at Lila's house because Fritzy was short and fat and wore nothing but loose, flowered mumu dresses. Mom was tall and thin and dressed elegantly. Everyone in the neighborhood thought that Mom looked like a movie star. "Who needs Elizabeth Taylor when I got my own here?" Dad always said with pride.

Sometimes I got the courage to speak up and say "no" to Lila. She never liked that. Her face would scrunch up and she would strike back, hurting me. The worst was when she said, "We got switched at birth and your mom was really mine and Fritzy was yours." The first time she said that to me, I got so upset I wet my pants. Lila loved that; she delighted in it. I ran into the bathroom to change and when I came back into the bedroom, I started to point and poke my finger at the parts of her body where Lila's eczema was showing. Her skin wasn't as bad as Fritzy's; it came and went but when it popped up, it was ugly. Lila almost always wore long sleeves to cover it up, even when it was summer.

"Oh, yeah, Lila, well how come you and your mother have the same scabby skin and my mom and I don't? There's not a mark on us!"

Lila got furious. She slapped one hand over my mouth and with the other pinched and twisted the skin on the inside of my thighs. At moments like that, I prayed to God for Mom to walk in. I wanted her to see that Lila was not the beautiful girl with the face of an angel that everyone saw, but that she really was the devil with a heart to match.

When we were eight years old, we both started dance lessons. I went to a studio in my neighborhood in the Bronx, but Max felt it wasn't good enough for Lila because she was going to be famous one day. Every Saturday he took her to a studio in Manhattan. "Nothing but the best for my girl," he bragged.

For a while on Friday nights, after our parents finished playing cards, we held a mini-recital. As always, Lila took charge. It was my job to move the furniture and play the part of the announcer. Lila was so conniving. She'd show up with an introduction she had written the night before. Then she would tap dance her nasty little heart away to "Alexander's Rag Time Band." By the time she finished her routine and our parents stopped clapping and praising her, the night was over. Fritzy would start yawning, and Max would say that Lila needed her beauty rest. I never, ever got a chance to show off my routine, ever!

Since our birthdays were on the same day, we celebrated them together at China Moon. It was on our eleventh birthday, after the ice cream mound with fruit and sparklers, that Lila spoke softly in my ear that she had a surprise for me at the next card night.

The following Friday, Lila steered me into her bedroom and made me stand in front of the full - length mirror on her door. She stood beside me and we stared at ourselves. "What are we doing?" I asked.

"Notice anything different about us?" Lila asked.

I took a long look at myself and then at Lila. It was pretty obvious that we both had physically changed, but each in different ways. A few weeks before, much to my surprise, I discovered, overnight, that I had developed breasts. They were large enough to make me a constant target for bra snapping by Sammy Roth, the class clown. Lila's breasts were small, round, with real nipples. I didn't have any nipples and Lila loved to make cracks about it whenever she could. She called hers "cherries" and mine “the pits." She thought it was hilarious. I was also still short and a bit chubby. Lila had lost all her baby fat and grown three inches. All the boys in school had a crush on her and all the girls were jealous of her.

"So my titties are big, what about it?"

"Nothing. Lots of boys like them like that," she said.

"OK, so is there a reason why we're standing here like the Bobbsey twins?" I asked sarcastically.

"Sarah, look at us; we're totally opposite each other in the looks department. But, we are both really pretty and the boys are staring at us. It's time for us to step up and take our place as the most popular girls in school. We need to be ready. Seventh grade, eighth grade, and, before you know it, we’ll be in high school. Remember, practice makes perfect. The Spring Dance is coming up in three weeks, so the time to start is now!"

"And how do we do that, Miss Know-it-all?"

Lila took me by the hand and sat me down on the bed. "By

playing our new game. Now, lesson one is how to kiss the boys and make them never forget."

"But, what if I don't want to kiss anybody?"

"Not even Kenny Schwartz? I know you like him. Come on, just close your eyes and pretend I'm Kenny." I had no idea how she knew about Kenny; I hadn't told anyone. But then again Lila managed some way to find out everything about me.

As always, Lila was in charge and just as if she were directing a movie, she lay down on the bed and instructed me to lie beside her. To make me less nervous, Lila began to tickle me. For a few minutes, we acted like silly young girls, giggling and making faces. When she started to kiss me, I knew it was wrong but I liked it. We went on like that for a while and then her kisses turned from gentle to rough. Her hand moved over my body, touching different places. Her eczema had popped up and her hands were red and chapped. I didn't like them on me. I tried to back away but that made her angry. Instead of pinching my thighs, she went for my breasts.

"Just lie still, Sarah, it's going to feel good, I promise."

I closed my eyes shut. As if she were playing the piano, Lila's fingers maneuvered their way over my belly and down to my thighs and ended up underneath my panties. Lila took three of her fingers and gently fondled me in my most private place. I instantly trembled.

"I told you," she said with amusement. "Now, you do me."

I immediately panicked. I felt ashamed. I wanted to throw up. Then it all turned. Lila pushed me away and stared at me with disgust as if I had initiated the game. I just wanted to crawl into a hole. Lila got off the bed, straightened her hair, her clothes, and pointed a finger at me.

"Just remember, Sarah, not a word. If you tell your parents, I'll say it was all your idea and you made me do all those awful things. Who do you think they will believe?"

Lila left the bedroom, not happy.

I went straight to the bathroom and took my clothes off, splashed cold water all over me, praying that the shame I felt would wash away.

While I got dressed, I heard Lila in the kitchen, joking with my parents. When I finished, I went straight into the living room. Not able to face my parents, I sat down and turned on the TV.

"Sweetheart, you all right?" my mom shouted out.

"Fine, Mom," I answered, hoping that she would leave me alone.

For the rest of the night, Lila and I sat on opposite ends of the couch, watching Friday night comedy shows. She laughed. I didn't. When Fritzy and Max were ready to leave, Lila got up and put her arms around me and whispered, "Not a word."

Our Spring Dance came and went and nothing happened. Kenny never even made it to the dance because he got the measles. The only boy that paid me any attention was Sammy Roth, my devoted bra-snapper, who was a loser. The whole evening was awful.

The practice session hadn't done me any good, but it did pay off for Lila. All the boys wanted to dance with her. She disappeared for a while during the dance, once with Ernie Littman and once with Carmine Rossi, and who knows who else. I didn't care.

Because of one thing or another, I found excuses for not being around on card nights and apparently Lila did, too. Except for school, we hardly saw each other and that was fine with me. One night I wasn't so lucky and ended up having to stay home. Mom told me that Lila was coming also. Max had news to tell us.

When they walked in, Lila and Max entered first, filled with excitement, with Fritzy, behind them looking blank-faced. Max had bought a bottle of whiskey and poured a glass for him and my parents, not for Fritzy. She was not allowed to drink.

"Dear Hannah and Leo, I am sorry to say that our Friday night card game has come to an end. Leo, you will have to find someone else to take money from," said Max with humor. "Lila has been invited to be part of an advanced dance class in her studio and, unfortunately, it is held on Friday nights. This is a great opportunity for my precious Lila. It is the beginning of the road to her future. My Lila is destined to be a big star."

Mom and Dad clapped their hands and congratulated Lila

with hugs and kisses. Fritzy remained silent. It was as if she weren't a part of any of it. Me, I could hardly believe what I had just heard. Daddy got up and raised his glass to make a toast.

"To you, Lila, may all your dreams come true. My family wishes you great success. But you better remember to give us free tickets when you are on the stage! Now, Max, let's play cards, and tonight I might even let you win, so you can pay for all these fancy lessons!"

After supper, Lila made a gesture pointing to my bedroom. "One last time," Lila said.

I pretended not to hear her and walked into the living room. I felt her disappointment and anger as she followed me. I turned on the TV, took a handful of peanuts from a bowl, and made myself comfortable. I was ecstatic! That night we watched our usual shows, but the only one of us that laughed was me. The Friday night games were finally over.

Part One

1959

September - December

September

Sarah

Sarah Meets Mr. Dudley

"Come on, Sarah, rise, and shine. Mr. Dudley will be here at 8:00."

"Coming, Mom," I shout out.

I walk into the kitchen and there is Mom, looking like she just stepped out of a *Madamoiselle Magazine* cover shot: slim black skirt, wide black patent leather belt, white tailored blouse, black patent leather pumps, and her pearl earrings.

"Wow, you look just like a fashion model!"

"Well, thank you but . . . is that what you are wearing this morning?"

I look down at my shirt and capris and shrug my shoulders.

"I . . . yes. Why?"

Mom gives out a big sigh, comes to me and kisses me on the head.

"Sweetheart, do me a favor and go change into that new blue sweater set I bought you and the navy skirt. Please."

"OK, but why are we getting so dressed up? No one is going to see us. We'll be in the car."

"Sarah, trust me, the whole building is downstairs already. Today is a big deal and I want all of us should look nice. Besides, I have asked Mr. Dudley to take a picture of me behind the wheel and then one of the three of us. Oh, Sarah - I don't think I have been so excited since the day you were born. Now go sweetie, and change."

"Leo, come already, hurry up, don't make me late for my first driving lesson."

Ten minutes later, we're downstairs and, sure enough, it looks like all of 3335 DeKalb Avenue is waiting for us. I can't believe my eyes. There are people sitting on the steps of the building, some are seated in beach chairs on the sidewalk, others are standing around looking up and down the street as if they are waiting for a parade to come through. Even Juan, our Super, his wife Rosita and their six kids are part of the crowd. There is a small card table set up with a white tablecloth. On top are paper plates with Danishes, paper cups, two thermoses of coffee, two plastic pitchers filled with grape juice, and white napkins that have small American flags in red, white and blue printed on them.

Minnie and Selma, the twin spinsters and the chief yentas of the block, are leaning out from their windows.

"Look everyone, here she is," Minnie and Selma shout out.

Then all at once, there are cheers and everyone is waving at Mom.

"Mazel tov Hannah," someone yells.

Mrs. Lebow walks up to Mom, takes her hands, and holds them.

"You make us look good Hannah."

"Hey, Mrs. Lanin, you gonna do great," says Juan.

"Here she is, Miss America." sings Angel, Juan's oldest son.

Mom is right. This is a big deal. If she passes the driver's test, then she will be the first woman on our block to drive a car. I'm so proud of her. She is the best of the best. She is not only the prettiest Mom on the block, AND in the whole neighborhood, but she is also the nicest, like with a capital N. She listens to people, she cares about them. She does things for others when they are sick, even without their asking.

“Hey," someone shouts. I look around and my eyes gaze up at the second floor window.

There's Fritzy, looking mean as always. I don't think I have ever seen her smile. Lila is behind her.

“Remember, Sarah," Mom whispers to me, “it is not so easy living with a woman whose heart is made of stone."

For a little bitsy second, I feel sorry for Lila but . . . only for a second.

Meanwhile, Fritzy is leaning out her window so far that her humongous breasts are practically swinging over the window ledge.

“Hey Leo,” she yells, loud enough so that everyone can hear her. “How come it ain't you learning to drive?" Fritzy snickers.

“Shat, shat,” Minnie and Selma shout.

Fritzy ignores them, looks down on the street, and then glares right at Mom. When Fritzy gets like this, her whole face changes, her eyes narrow to small slits, and she does this thing with her mouth and lips where she squeezes them so tight that you think, any minute she's going to explode.

“Yeah, Leo, I guess now the whole neighborhood knows who wears the pants in your family.” This time Fritzy lets out a huge belly laugh.

No one says a word. Some of the neighbors look up and sneer, some turn away. Dad looks up at Fritzy.

“Fritzy, Fritzy, always, your mouth is moving faster than your brain. What, you still angry you lost at cards the other night? Doesn't matter, but you got this picture all wrong. See, if it’s Hannah that does the driving, then I got myself a damn good-looking chauffeur."

Dad then takes Mom into his arms, giving her a bear hug. Then he - oh no, - lays one of his big fat sloppy kisses on Mom’s mouth. She blushes and pushes him away but I can see she is loving it. Dad turns to everyone and raises his hands high in the air.

“Am I right people, or am I right?”

Everyone goes crazy and applauds! Fritzy slams her window shut, leaving Lila alone, staring down at us. Then in a blink of an eye, she's gone.

Meanwhile Howie Roth and his pals are jumping up and down, pointing at a two-tone gold and white shiny Buick coming slowly down the street. We all watch as the car glides up to the front of our building and stops. Howie and his friends go wild, running around the car howling like wild Indians.

"Check . . . it . . . out," Howie says, like he has just seen the most beautiful girl in the world and gives one long, slow whistle.

"Now that's a set of wheels, oh yeah!"

There isn't one person here that isn't staring at this car, with their eyes popping out.

I don't get it. Sure it's pretty but it is just a car. Oh, wait . . . the car door is opening and out steps a man. Not just any man, but a Negro with skin the color of chocolate syrup. Everyone is so surprised you can hear a pin drop. I have never seen anyone like him and I bet no one else here has either. His clothes make my eyes twitch. He's wearing a shirt with small and large red and pink polka dots, his pants are navy blue with white stripes, his shoes are red leather, and on his head is a white pork pie hat. My eyes dart all over the place, up, down, sideways. For a second I imagine that the polka dots are going to bounce off his shirt and bop us all on the head, just like in a cartoon.

Then it clicks in my head! Oh my God - this has got to be Mr. Dudley and he's . . . a Negro! Mr. Dudley takes his hat off and, just like in the movies, gallantly bows to the crowd.

When his head comes back up, he looks up at Minnie and Selma and greets them with another bow. He walks over to Dad and Mom and shakes their hands. He reaches out for mine and gives me a gigantic smile that shows . . . two gold teeth!

"You must be Miss Sarah and, if I say so myself, you are as beautiful as your Mother."

I know I'm supposed to be polite and say something but my mouth feels like it's filled with marbles. I'm so embarrassed. Everyone will talk for days. I look around; to my surprise, everyone is staring at me, and not at Mr. Dudley. I want to die, just die!

"Sarah," Mom asks, "can you say hello to Mr. Dudley, or have you lost your tongue?" I can't look at her. Tears fill my eyes, it's like everything is a blur. The next thing I know I am running away as fast as I can up the stairs. Mom grabs my arm from behind and we both enter the building and head into the hallway off the lobby. Tears fall from her eyes . . . then she slaps my face!

"This is for making me ashamed!" Then she slaps me again. "This is for you being so cruel to another human being!"

She is furious, her face is burning with anger; my cheeks are on fire, but I don't care! I'm just in shock.

"What is wrong with you? How can you shame me and Daddy like this?"

"But, Mom, why didn't you tell me he was a Negro? I was so embarrassed and his clothes, my God, he's . . ."

"What? What bothers you more, that he is a Negro or the kind of clothes he wears?"

I start to tell her but she puts her hand over my mouth . . . then Mom breaks down.

"Sarah, it has always been important for Daddy and me to teach you to not to turn away from people because of the color of their skin or what religion they believe in. Daddy and I have lost and suffered too much to ever look down on anyone. Now, we will both go back outside and you will apologize to Mr. Dudley and tell him how happy you are to meet him. Then I would like you to stay home and think about what I have said. When I come home, we will talk more. BUT, Sarah, I swear, if I ever see you do something like this again, to anyone, it will be more than a slap in the face that I give you. Do you understand?"

I nod, yes, but keep my head down because I'm afraid to see her disappointment in me.

The first thing I hear when I come out of the building is people laughing. They are listening to Mr. Dudley tell a story. It's like he has always been here. Even Minnie and Selma have come down to join the other neighbors and are feeding him cookies. As soon as Mr. Dudley sees me, he comes right up to me. I put out my hand.

"Mr. Dudley, I am pleased to make your acquaintance."

"Miss Sarah, the pleasure is all mine."

Mom gives me a quiet hug. Mr. Dudley holds open the car door and Mom slips carefully into the driver's seat. Dad goes in the backseat and Mr. Dudley sits next to Mom. She takes a few seconds to get comfortable and before I can ask if I can please come, the car drives away. No one says a word to me as I turn and go back into the building.

Lila

Watching From The Window

As soon as Daddy left this morning, Mom took her usual place at the living room window, sitting and watching the neighbors set up outside, getting ready to wish Hannah good luck. Mom already warned me last night that I wasn't allowed to go downstairs. And if I knew what was good for mc, I'd better not tell Daddy.

"If Hannah, the big shot, wants to make her husband look like a fool, that's his problem. But we are not going to be a part of it," she said with her usual nastiness.

At eight, I walk into the living room, where Mom is stationed, leaning out the window as far as she can so that she can't miss a thing. Sipping her coffee and sucking on her licorice candies, she tells me to stand behind her. Since Mom's body is wide enough to fill the window, I can't see much. But I can hear everyone rooting for Hannah. Right away I'm green with envy. I should be down there too, beside Hannah. Me, not, Sarah.

As the street fills up with Hannah's well-wishers, Mom gets more and more irritated by the second. By the time Hannah, Leo, and Sarah come out of the building, she's ready to attack. She waits till Hannah is on the street surrounded by her friends then yells out her first insult. But Leo is quick to answer back and has the whole crowd laughing on his side. I can't make out what he'd said, but there's no doubt that he's put Mom in her place. She's so angry that, when she gets up, the coffee cup and dish of candies fly off the window sill and her chair is knocked over. Grunting and muttering, she stomps out of the room, screaming at me to close the window. As soon as she goes into the bedroom, I pick up the coffee cup, dish, and candies and put them in the kitchen. When I come back, I take Mom's place at the window. I move the curtain over my face just a bit so no one can see me.

When I look down on the street, I'm blown away to see a Negro man dressed liked a clown giving Hannah a kiss on the cheek. Sarah looks like she's freaking out. All eyes are on Sarah, the Negro, and Hannah. Seconds pass by and nothing happens. It's like Sarah is supposed to be doing something but I don't know what. Suddenly Hannah grabs hold of Sarah and pulls her away and pushes her into the building. When Hannah comes out minutes later, she looks unhappy. Then Sarah comes out and shakes hands with the Negro and says something to him. The Negro smiles at her, and he, Hannah and Leo get into the car. It's not until Hannah starts the car and slowly drives away that everyone starts to talk to one another. From where I'm sitting, it sounds like a swarm of bees has taken over the block. I notice then that Sarah is already gone.

Sarah must have done something bad for Hannah to leave her behind, but when Hannah comes home, I'll be waiting for her. Yes, that's what I'll do. I'm going to sit right here till she comes back. Then she'll know who really appreciates and loves her.

Michael

Michael's Morning

Mother sits on my bed, her hands move gently through my hair; she is humming a German tune. She sounds happy. I rub my eyes with my fists. I'm almost afraid to open them and discover that it's all a dream. I take a deep breath. OK, here goes nothing! I open my eyes and there she is smiling. To my surprise, there is a tray on her lap.

"Good morning, my love, I have made your favorite breakfast - German apple cake, sausages, eggs, and a hot cup of cocoa."

I stare at the food in front of me and then at Mother. Breakfast in bed was always served only on my birthday. Mother would sit with me and we would read the newspapers together. She always planned something special for us to do on that day, a Broadway show downtown, a concert, or sometimes we would just see movies, two or three at a time, and then end up in Chinatown for dinner. Once, we went to the circus but we had to keep that secret from father. He would definitely not have approved.

But today isn't my birthday; it's just an ordinary Saturday. For a long time, Saturday was the best day of the week. Mother would meet me after my violin lesson and we would spend the day together, walk through the park, and have ice cream at the fountain. I love those days but we have not had one like that for a while.

Mother hasn't been well for the last few weeks. She has been getting sad again. When this happens, she stays in bed all day. Somehow she manages to get up and have supper and the table set in time for Father when he comes home from work.

Supper is always hard for me. I get nervous. Except for Father asking his routine questions about my day at school, lessons, and practice, and Mother asking how his day went we say little else. That is unless Father has had a bad day and then he goes on and on how he hates having to work side by side with a bunch of ignorant refugees. By this, he means Jewish refugees, the ones who came from Europe and were in the concentration camps. I hate it when he talks like this because Mother is Jewish, and she spent a year in the camps. We are from Europe, so that makes us like them, doesn't it?

I haven't seen Mother cheerful like this for weeks. Her dark moods come and go and take her away from me, sometimes for an hour, sometimes for days, sometimes longer. I don't know what makes today different, but I'm so happy to have her back. I've missed her.

Mother announces that she is coming with me to my lesson. Afterwards we will go out to lunch and then who knows. "I feel like all things are possible today!"

I stare at her and realize that I haven't said a word since she came in, that Mother has been doing all the talking. Later, walking out of the building, we're surprised there is a crowd of adults and children spilling out onto the sidewalk. For a minute I think there has been an accident, but then I hear Mother giggling.

"Oh, Michael, I wonder if this is what is called a block party. So many people . . . they must all be neighbors. Everyone seems so excited! And oh my, look, over there," she says. Her finger is pointing to a Negro man standing in front of a sleek, white and gold car. "Have you ever seen anything so wonderful?"

I don't know what to say. I'm kind of dazzled by everything

I'm seeing. But Mother is right, the car is beautiful and the man is dressed in an outfit that is extraordinary! The two of us have not moved from where we are. It's as if we are hypnotized by all that we see.

The Negro tips his hat to the crowd and introduces himself. He then walks up to Sarah Lanin and her parents. I know Sarah from school but we've never spoken to each other. She looks overwhelmed at the sight of the Negro. He shakes Mr. Lanin's hand and then surprises everyone by kissing Mrs. Lanin on the cheek. The adults are caught by surprise and become quiet. Sarah steps back from her mother and the Negro. She looks like she wants to be anywhere but here. As the Negro approaches her with a big smile, Sarah retreats even further from him. The expression on her mother's face is one of shock and embarrassment. Suddenly Mrs. Lanin takes Sarah by the arm and ushers her into the building. The adults start to whisper.

When Mrs. Lanin comes back outside, her husband puts his arm around her waist and whispers something in her ear. Sarah comes out of the building and shakes hands with the Negro. The Negro and Mr. and Mrs. Lanin get into the car, we hear the sound of the engine starting, the car slowly pulls away and drives down the street, and Sarah walks back into the building. As the crowd breaks up, I turn around and I look up to the second floor in Sarah's building. There is a girl standing behind a closed window. I have seen her at school. Her name is Lila. All the boys love her and all the girls hate her. I wonder why she isn't down here with everyone else.

Mother takes my hand and squeezes it. She's still so excited by everything that I don't think she's aware of what just took place. "Michael, we must get out more and mingle. Our neighbors seem like very fine people." Mother says this with such confidence that I believe today may be a special day. We are about to leave when a heavy hand comes down on my shoulder. I know immediately it is Father. I look at Mother and see that his other hand is around her waist.

He puts his head between the two of us so tight that we cannot move. His voice is soft but threatening, "So this is where the two of you disappeared to. Hmm . . . and here you are, watching these people, and who is that Negro? This neighborhood is bad enough without the likes of them." Father turns and looks straight at Mother. "I am very disappointed in you, Judith. I would think that since this is the earliest you have gotten up in the last few weeks that you could find better things to do with your time. As for you, Michael, you can use your time for extra practice. Your recital is in two weeks. Later today, we will go to the store and get you a new shirt."

I can feel Mother's spirit fade away. If I were to look at her eyes right now, I would see that all the joy of this morning has disappeared.

Sarah

Sarah's Mother Tells A Story

Mom is beaming, holding a bouquet of flowers.

"Sarah, your mother is not only beautiful and smart, but she's gonna be a hell of a driver," says Dad, filled with pride.

Dad takes the flowers and waltzes into the kitchen to put them in a vase. Mom sits down on the couch, takes her shoes off, and puts her feet up on the coffee table. She pats the seat next to her for me to come to her. Right away, I tell her how sorry I am. "Sarah, I think it's time I tell you about an experience that may help you understand." She holds me close to her and for the next hour tells me about the day that she was liberated from the concentration camp.

"One morning in the camps, instead of being woken up for roll call by shouting Kapos and dogs and being poked with boots, the women and I were surprised by a strange silence. All of us looked at each other, wondering what was going on. Afraid that the Nazis were playing a joke on us, we stayed where we were and waited for something to happen. After a while, one by one, we walked outside. The camp was empty. Not knowing what to do, too scared to run, we sat on the ground and waited. To this day, I'm not sure how long it was till the American Army came into the camp and liberated us. At first, we did not believe what the soldiers were telling us. Then a hand reached out to me, a brown hand. I looked up and saw my first Negro. I had seen Negroes in American movies but never in person. He lifted me up from the ground and carried me as tenderly as if I were a newborn baby. With his tears falling down on my face, he told me that I was safe, the War was over. So you see, Mr. Dudley being a Negro never made a difference to me or Daddy and it shouldn't for you. When you see Mr. Dudley next time, be as kind to him as he is to us. Now, because I was such a good student today, Daddy is taking us to China Moon late."

During dinner, Dad can't stop talking about the driving lesson. His excitement and pride are contagious. When we get back home, I ask Mom if we could stay out a little longer. She looks at Dad.

"Sure, you two stay down and schmooze. Me, I'm gonna have a nightcap and go to bed. What a day," he says, with a wink and a smile.

The street is empty. We make ourselves comfortable and sit quietly. In my head, I have a hundred questions for Mom about the war. I want to hear more stories. Today when she told me about being liberated, it was like listening to another person. There is so much I don't know about her and Dad.

"Hmm, I can see you are busy thinking. What more do you want to know?"

OK here goes! I'm ready to ask my first question when I hear an angry voice from a distance. I jump up and look left and right to see where it's coming from. Mom hears it too, but she pulls me back and orders me to sit down.

"Shush! It is Mr. Stein and his son Michael. When they walk by us, make believe you did not hear anything," Mom says, seriously.

Before I sit, I sneak another look. I can see Mr. Stein clearly. He looks really aggravated. It's hard to make out Michael's reaction from where I am, but, when he brushes his hair from his eyes, it is again crystal clear how unbelievably handsome he is. Tall, thin, with wide shoulders - he looks like a teen idol.

Michael and his parents moved into the building next door to us about a year ago. His mother and father don't mix with anyone. Once in a while, I see him and his mother walk together to the park. She's almost as beautiful as Mom but in a different way. Dad tried talking to Mr. Stein once on the subway coming home from work. I don't know what happened, but Dad came home cursing him in Yiddish so I couldn't understand everything.

Michael and I are both in the seventh grade. I've never talked to him and he doesn't hang out with anyone. But everyone in school knows that Michael plays the violin. The word is that he's supposed to be some kind of musical genius. I've heard him play at school concerts.

Although I've never told anyone, including my best friend Roxy, I have a little secret. Michael's bedroom window is directly across from mine. I can hear him practice his violin. I always keep my shades down because I don't want him thinking I'm a peeping tom. Not that it matters, because I'm sure he doesn't even know I exist. Oh, here they come: they're walking right by us! Mom pulls me back by my collar and we try to make ourselves invisible. Once they pass by us and enter their building, I ask Mom what she knows about them.

"Not much. I hear they came from Germany after the War, settled in New Jersey, and then came here. Sometimes I see her at the butcher's and say hello. She gives a little shy smile and walks away. And you know that Daddy doesn't like him at all."

"I think Michael is lonely. I'm going to say hello to him tomorrow. He looks like he could use a friend . . . What do you think, Mom?"

"That is very sweet of you, but you should be careful. Don't be too pushy."

And that is when I decide to make Michael Stein my best friend.

Michael

That Same Evening

I've made him angry. Father hasn't stopped scolding me since we left the clothing store. All I did was ask for a pair of dungarees. My clothes are always the same - long sleeved, white shirts for the fall and winter, short sleeved, white shirts for the spring and summer; two pairs of navy blue pants, two pairs of gray pants, and a pair of brown oxford shoes.

As soon as we leave the store, Father starts in on one of his lectures, reminding me who I am. I've heard this speech so often that I can recite every word by heart. "You are the son of Joseph Stein, and at no time are you to ever imitate the current style or identify with the boys in this neighborhood. They are beneath you. They all run wild in the streets like animals. They have no manners or respect. Always remember, Michael, we, you, are different from the others who live here, and you and your mother must behave accordingly. Do not worry. I promise that one day I will take the three of us away from here!"

It doesn't do any good to argue with him or stand up to him because he'll only punish me later and then maybe Mother, too. I hate him.

Just before we get to our building, I see out of the corner of my eye two people sitting on the stoop of the building before mine. It's Sarah Lanin and her mother. I pretend not to notice them and pray that they cannot hear what Father is saying. I wish I could disappear right this second.

Sarah

The Park

It's Saturday and I have nothing to do. As usual, Mom is taking her driving lesson with Dudley, Dad is working overtime at the factory, Roxy is visiting her grandparents, and I am alone.

By now, the neighborhood has gotten used to the fact that Mom is doing this, so it's not such a big deal anymore No one calls him Mr. Dudley anymore, it's just plain Dudley. Everyone likes him so much. Even Minnie and Selma come down on Saturday mornings, always carrying a treat they have baked especially for him. Being the charmer he is, he takes an extra few minutes and fills them with compliments. I bet Dudley is probably the most popular man on our block. The ones that still do not talk to him are Lila and Fritzy. Max works on Saturday mornings, so he's never met him.

Well, it's eleven o'clock and no one is going to be home till three. Might as well go to Harry's Soda Shoppe, buy an egg cream and the new Teen Magazine. I change into my new capris, a white sleeveless shirt, and my new Keds. I look at myself in the mirror and decide I am definitely cute - even adorable. Who knows, today I might run into Kenny, my heartthrob, or, even better, Michael Stein?

The first person I see when I walk into Harry's is Lila. To

make matters worse, she's standing at the magazine rack, next to Kenny, all cuddly. They're looking at a magazine and laughing at something. I could just kill her. I make a turnabout and am ready to leave, when Harry waves at me and tells me to come and sit down. Too late! Lila and Kenny see me and Lila gives me a big grin.

"Hey, what's your hurry, Missy? You just got here," laughs Harry.

He tells me to sit down and have an egg cream, his treat. "So how's your momma? You know, Sarah, if I didn't like your father so much, I'd steal her from him in a minute."

Pretending I don't see Lila and Kenny, I sit myself down on the stool. I know any second now she's going to do something to make my day "crap."

"So, sweetheart, I hear that your momma is doing real good. Bet she gets her license in no time. In the meantime, my Ida can't stop talking about learning to drive. She wants Dudley to teach her. I tell her she's crazy; she can't even ride a bike."

Harry is so pleased with his own joke that the other customers at the counter all laugh along with him. I can't smile. I stare down at my egg cream but don't have the stomach for it now. I jump off the stool, thank Harry, tell him I don't feel well, and start to leave, when Lila and Kenny come right in front of me. Kenny, the boy I never got to speak to, never got to kiss, is holding Lila's hand.

"Well, look who's here," says Lila. "I thought you'd be with your mom and Dudley. I can't believe your father would let the two of them be alone. It's not right." Lila leans into me and says just loud enough for everyone to hear, "You know people are talking."

I want to kill her, stomp on her, hurt her. If Mom knew what Lila had just said, she would be so hurt. Harry comes around from behind the counter and walks right up to Lila and tells her she should be ashamed of herself. But Lila doesn't seem to be bothered by Harry at all. Instead she goes at me again.

"I'm only repeating what I hear; that's all."

That's it. I have to shut her up. I take my unfinished egg cream and dump it all over the front of her blouse. Lila goes nuts.

"Now, Lila, you and everyone else can talk about this,

instead."

By the time I reach the end of the block, I can still hear Lila cursing at me. Now I'm feeling good. I'm going to walk to the Park and maybe I'll find someone nice to hang out with.

Michael

Michael Meets Sarah

Today is not a good day. I can't concentrate. After twenty minutes, Maestro Franco waves his hand in the air and says, "Michael, please, put your violin down! Come sit down on the couch." I sit and look up at my teacher.

"You look pale today. Your music, I am sorry to say, sounds *cosi stanco*. Close your eyes, rest a while. I go and have Signora make you an espresso with a little milk, a sugar cube, and something a little special. Then I want you to go home. *Capisce*?"

Maestro Franco leaves, singing out his wife's name, Gabriella, letting her know he is coming into the kitchen. Instead of closing my eyes, I do what I love best when I come here. I gaze at the paintings on the walls, the tall stacks of books that seem to be everywhere, the stained glass lamps that surround the room with soft light, and the overstuffed couch and chairs with colorful velvet shawls draped over them. The room is filled with pictures of his and the Signora's family from Italy and their five daughters.

Maestro always talks about how much he loves his daughters. "God has chosen to give me only angels! I will need to have one hundred students to be able to pay for all their weddings! Should I be angry at him or should I bless him for the privilege to be surrounded by beauty all day?" When he is finished with his loving complaints, he throws kisses at the photos of them with pride and love. Then he winks at me. "Who knows, Michael, maybe one day, you will choose to fall in love with one of my *belle donne* and you will ask for her hand! But not until you become a famous violinist. A poor musician for a son-in-law, I cannot afford!"

When Maestro Franco comes back, he enters the living room with the Signora, carrying a tray with small cups and a plate of cannoli, my favorite. Signora Gabriella sits down next to me and places her hand on my forehead.

"Franco, this boy feels warm! After he eats, you send him home. Here Michael, I just baked these. *Mangia* and I have some for you to take home to your beautiful Mama."

"*Mi scusi,* Gabriella, what you think? I am not sensitive to my best pupil? I already told him he could go home. Right, Michael?" I nod affirmatively. "Women! They think only they can feel!"

As I am getting ready to leave, Maestro Franco lifts my chin and looks me straight in the eye. "Your mama, we no see her the last few weeks, she is OK?"

I'm too embarrassed to tell him the truth. "Yes, she just has a bad cold."

"I am sorry. Please, you be sure you let her know that Signora and I miss our little chats. *Ciao*, see you next week."

Once I started to tell Maestro about Mother, but I didn't know how to explain what happens to her when she gets sad. Sometimes her sadness is so bad that she can't do anything but go into her room and sleep. There are days I only see her in the morning and when she makes supper. We eat together but she mostly watches me and asks about how my day was. By the time I am finished, her plate is still full and I know that she really didn't listen to me at all. Her mind was somewhere else. I help Mother clean up; she kisses me good night and goes into her bedroom.

When she leaves me, I feel very lonely.

The only good thing that comes out of Mother's dark moods is that Father chooses to work late. I don't think he likes to see her that way any more than I do and, by the time he comes home, I am asleep and avoid having to be questioned by him about what I did or did not do.

But, when Mother is well, she comes to my violin lesson and listens with pride. Then she and the Maestro and the Signora have their talks. She loves to hear about Italy and asks many questions. After sweets and coffee, we sometimes go to the movies. We always see musicals or comedy.

"Don't you wish we could just jump up and fly right into the screen and, like magic, we become part of the movie like it was our real lives. Wouldn't that be wonderful, Michael? Just the two of us!"

She is so happy on these days that she even talks about her friends and family before the war. Then her eyes start to water and her smile and laugh disappear. No one in her family except for her survived the concentration camps in Germany. She does not talk about it.

My parents were married when all of this happened, but Father was not taken to the camps because he is not Jewish. But, here in America, no one is supposed to know that. It is a secret. My parents and I do not have any friends. No one comes over. There is no one to notice that we do not attend synagogue. If it were not for Mr. Adams, my music teacher at school, and the Maestro and his *Signora*, I sometimes feel that no one would even know I exist.

But Father wants it this way. He is always suspicious of other people. When something goes wrong at work, he is always blaming the Jews. When he comes home, he gives the same speech over and over again. "If the Jews in the neighborhood should find out that I am not of them, they will want to make my life miserable. They think all Germans are Nazis. This is, of course, not true. After all, I tried very hard to save your mother and her parents from the camps. I did everything I could, but, unfortunately, it was impossible. After the war, I searched for your mother in every DP camp in Germany. Right, Judith? Tell the boy."

Mother never answers him; she just stops what she is doing

and walks out of the room. Once, when Mother and I were alone, I asked her about what Father said.

"What does he mean when he says he tried but could not save you or your parents? Why not?"

"Michael, I do not want to talk about these things, ever. Maybe one day, when you are older, but not now."

I do not ask anymore.

When I said goodbye this morning, Mother went straight into her bedroom. I am sure she is probably still there, so there is no rush to get home. It is a nice day. I will walk to the park and maybe sketch something.

I take a seat on the bench across from the fountain. I put my violin and cannoli down and see a little girl and boy splashing water at each other — their mother smiling as she watches them playing and giggling. I try to remember if I ever played like that when I was little, but I can't.

When I left Mother today, she hardly looked at me. I wonder if she even loves me anymore. Maybe coming here wasn't such a good idea. Watching the kids makes me feel worse. I should leave, but where would I go?

As I start to daydream again about running away, when I hear loud voices. I turn and see Howie Rothman and his gang of four coming in my direction. They're always looking for trouble. I stay out of their way at school so they don't really bother me, but today I fear I may not be so lucky. My eyes roam around the fountain, the kids and their mothers leaving. I keep looking and I spot a girl from my school, Lila Rosen. She's in the same grade as me, 7th. I think she's twelve but looks older. She's beautiful and self-confident but not very popular. The girls at school ignore her but the boys are always staring at her, hoping that she will notice one of them. The man she's walking with is her father. I recognize him because he comes to pick her up sometimes from school. I want to run up to them but they're almost out of the park, too.

Howie and his friends are getting close. I'll just pretend I don't see them. I pick up my violin and cannoli and cross my fingers. Maybe they'll just ignore me. I walk quickly and am just about at the gate when one of the boys jumps in front of me. The others circle around me. There are five of them.

"Hey, look who's here, guys. It's Michael, the musical hotshot," Howie says.

His friends move in closer. Before I know it, Howie snatches the paper bag from my hand, takes out a cannoli and stuffs it in his mouth. He takes out the second cannoli and finishes that, too. He crushes the bag and tosses it into the air.

"Mmm, these are out of sight! What other goodies you got for me, Michael? I could sure use a malted to wash down all that sugar. You got any money?"

If I did, I'd give it to him in a second, but I have nothing.

"I don't, but you know what, next time I see you, I'll treat you to one at Harry's — he makes the best malted in the neighborhood." Why am I saying this? Now he knows I'm scared.

"Well, I got to go, see you around."

Howie looks at his pals. They are so close to me I can smell them. "Hey, not so fast, Michael. How about you play us a tune on your violin. We'd like that, right guys?" Howie gives me a big grin and, before I know it, he snatches my case from me. He snaps open the locks on my case and removes the violin. I'm not sure what he is going to do, but I know I can't let him hurt my violin. I can't! Howie holds the violin and examines it, moving his fingers up and down the body of the violin from the tuning pegs down to the chin rest. One of the boys gets on his toes and dances, making like he's a ballerina. The boys chuckle. Howie plucks a string, closes his eyes, and brings the violin to chest. Then he does something so disgusting, my stomach turns. I watch in horror as Howie begins to lick my violin. I can see the wetness of his saliva dribbling down the wood.

"Please don't do that!" My voice cracks. Howie closes his eyes and dances with the violin as if it is a girl. By now the boys are howling and whistling, all at the same time.

"You know, Michael, this feels so nice and smooth, just like a sweet babe. Hey, you know, come to think of it, I've never seen you with a girl except, of course, your pretty momma."

He says this with a snicker and rubs his crotch. I've never hit anyone in my life but I need to do something. I tighten my fists as hard as I can and with all the strength I have, I lunge at Howie, aiming for his face, but I miss and hit his shoulder instead. Howie is so taken by surprise that he loses his balance, lands on his back, and drops the violin. I make a leap for it and grab it.

"Oh shit," says one of the boys. "This ain't good."

It's now or never and I start to make a run for it!

"Get the little fairy," Howie shouts out.

In seconds, two of the boys catch me, take hold of my arms, and force my hands behind my back. My violin drops to the ground. Howie gets himself up, struts up to me, spits in my face, raises both hands, and his knuckles are aiming for my face.

"Howie Rothman, you tell your moron turds to let him go, now!"

Howie turns around on a dime. The boys, including me, look around, left and right. Walking towards us, totally unafraid, is Sarah Lanin.

"What the hell, Sarah?" Howie scratches his head, looking stunned.

If I wasn't so scared, I would be laughing, but I am smart enough to know that would not be a good move right now.

"Howie, if your friends don't let him go this second, I swear I will kick you where the sun don't shine!"

She sounds so sure of herself that the boys drop me like a hot sack of potatoes. Howie squints his eyes at Sarah. I can see he's thinking what his next move is. Then double - quick, he spins around to his friends like he is dancing, winks at them, then takes a step back, does another turnabout, and raises his hands in the air.

"I give up, Sarah, I'm all yours." Howie breaks out into a big shit-eating grin.

"In your dreams, Bubba! Now give him back his violin and case!"

Howie is embarrassed at the way she's talking to him, especially in front of his friends. This is not cool so he can't let her win. He puts the violin back in the case and closes it but lets it lie next to his feet.

"Sarah, we're just having some fun. Right, Michael?"

"That's not what it looks like to me. I know you, you're just being a bully." Sarah glares at the other boys. "And that goes for all of you. Geez, you ought to be ashamed. You need five of you to gang up on one guy?"

Howie bites his lip, cracks his knuckles. He inches slowly up to Sarah, till they are nose to nose. Sarah does not move and looks downright fierce.

"Aw right, Sarah, time to go home," says Howie, clenching his teeth.

"If you say so, but when I get home should I tell your mother, who happens to be at my apartment this minute having coffee with my mother that you're beating someone up again? Mmm, I don't think so. What was it, three or four wooden spoons that she broke, hitting you over the head, the last time you did this?" Sarah asks.

Howie's face turns beet red. He is about to go berserk. "Stop butting in, Sarah. Go away or you'll be sorry," Howie threatens.

"Ok, now I'm scared." Sarah shakes her knees and mimics Howie.

Howie grunts, and his eyes dart back and forth from Sarah to me. He takes his foot and kicks my case as hard as he can. It slides several feet away from me.

"There's your case. Go ahead, Michael, or should I call you Michele?"

The other guys give out a nervous laugh. With a snap of his finger, Howie motions to his friends that they should leave. As they swagger away, each of them takes a turn kicking the violin case. Howie stops, raises his middle finger in the air, and shouts out, "You watch out, Sarah, next time I won't be so easy on you."

"I'll be sure to remember that, Howie," Sarah yells back.

I take a handkerchief from my pocket and gently wipe any evidence of Howie from my violin. I place the violin back in the case and close it.

"Is it okay?" Sarah asks.

"Yes. Thanks for what you did, I really appreciate it."

"No sweat. Howie is a cretin. Hey, you got time for a slice of pizza and a coke?"

I'm not sure what to say. I don't know how to talk to anyone, let alone a girl. Before I can give her a answer, Sarah takes me by the hand and leads me out of the park. Just as we get outside the gate, someone gives out a low whistle. We both turn around and sitting on a bench is Tommy DeMarco with his girlfriend BoBo. Tommy is in 8th grade. BoBo is in 7th, same as me. All the girls, even those who won't admit it, have a crush on him. All the boys who aren't part of his gang are afraid of him. He wears the same black leather motorcycle jacket, white T-shirt, and black tight jeans every day, and his black hair is greased, ending in a ducktail. BoBo dresses just like Tommy. His father owns a bakery one block away from Maestro Franco's building. Sometimes, I see Tommy working there. One time, when I passed by, he was standing outside and whistled at me. "Hey, you like playing the violin or your parents make you do that?"

From the sound of his voice, I couldn't tell if he was making fun of me or if he was serious.

"It started out that way. I have been playing for a while. I like it."

I was not sure if he was going to laugh at me or not, but he didn't. Instead, it looked like he was thinking about my answer. "Maestro Franco and the Mrs. come in here all the time. Maestro says you're a genius. You think you're a genius?"

"No, but I think I'm good."

"I like that. You're cool. Maybe one day, I'll hear you play."

I felt my cheeks go red. I couldn't believe this was happening. Tommy DeMarco called me cool. I wonder what he thinks of me now, after watching me being saved by a girl.

"You guys were OK back there. Howie is a knucklehead but it still took guts, two against five!"

"It was nothing, he doesn't scare me," says Sarah.

"Well, if he ever bothers the two of you again, I'll have a conversation with him that he won't forget."

"Thanks, Tommy, see you around and you, too, BoBo," Sarah says, sweetly.

"Hey, Sarah," said Tommy, "when you see your girlfriend, Lila, tell her I said hello." Sarah looks annoyed but she doesn't say anything. I can hear BoBo yelling at Tommy in the background.

October

Sarah
Tar Beach

I did it! Yeah! The last few weeks, my wish has come true. Micahel Stein and I have become best friends; it was *kismet*, meant to be. And tomorrow, I'm going to bring him to my special place, Tar Beach - that's the rooftop of my building. I know it sounds a little weird, but I love it. I have a whole beach setup there; the only thing missing is the sand and the water. And tomorrow will be the perfect day. The newspaper says it is supposed to be a scorcher, in the 90s, record-breaking for the month of October. What better time to go up there?

During the summer some of the neighbors use the rooftop to cool off on hot nights, but no one uses it during the day, so I have the place pretty much to myself - which is just the way I like it. I go up there a lot, even when it's not summer. It's a good place to read, dance like crazy, sing out loud, and daydream. Then there are the days when I feel like I'm on the verge of flipping out. I can go up there, jump up and down, and curse as loud as I want, which I am getting pretty good at. I know I'm only thirteen, but not everything is always easy for me. I get confused and frustrated about life and stuff, but up there I can try to think it out without anyone telling me if I'm wrong or right or that I should do this and not do that! Tar Beach is important to me. Mom and Dad kind of realize it, too, because they never complain about my going up there as much as I do.

Last year for my birthday, Dad surprised me with two beach chairs, two beach towels, a blanket, and a bright red transistor radio. It is just great, like my own living room in the sun. When they're not being used, I wrap everything up in plastic and put them in a special bin that Dad made for me to keep on the rooftop. This way they won't get rusty.

Of course, not everyone appreciates Tar Beach the way I do. Like when I brought Roxy up there for the first time. It was a hot summer day, and the sun was blazing. I covered us in my homemade suntan lotion - iodine, and olive oil - and we sat there soaking up the sun. A few hours later, I had to run down and get Mom, because Roxy, being a redhead with a thousand freckles, was as red as a lobster and so burnt that she couldn't move.

Thank God, Mom was home. Roxy was pretty hysterical and crying, and I didn't know what to do. Mom and I got Roxy to our apartment and very carefully put her down on my bed, where Mom massaged her with cold sour cream, and then placed wet towels on her body. My room smelled awful. Finally, after two hours, Roxy quieted down and we took her home.

Roxy's mother went ballistic when she saw her and immediately put her in bed and called Dr. Horowitz. As we were leaving, I could swear that Roxy's mom was giving me the evil eye. The next morning Mom called and was told that Roxy had sun poisoning and did not want to see me.

I could only stay away a day. I had to tell Roxy how sorry I was. When I walked into her bedroom, I wasn't ready for what I saw. Roxy was lying in bed covered from head to toe in some kind of paste and two wet teabags on her eyes. A giggle jumped from my throat and then more followed. I couldn't control myself. Well, that did it! Roxy sat up in bed, the paste cracking and crumbling all over the sheets, and took the wet tea bags off her eyes and threw them at me. After three weeks, Roxy forgave me and decided that she still could come up to Tar Beach but only when it was cloudy, and she would always wear a big hat. The other person who did not like the sun and had no interest in Tar Beach was Lila. Lucky me! But, as always, she had to see what I was up to. One day, she opened the door to the roof, took one look around, gazed up at the sun, and announced that this might be OK for me but, definitely not for her!

"You see, Sarah, when you have a face like mine, with skin so translucent and glowing, I can never, ever, be in the sun. It would be a crime to harm the perfection of my complexion. And, because I have chosen a future on the stage and screen, I must always be forever careful."

As I listened to her performing her little speech or, I should say, monologue, acting like she was Vivien Leigh in *Gone with the Wind*, even with the thickest southern accent there ever was, I had no choice but to crack up. I was laughing so hard, tears were running down my face. I thought Lila was going to have a nervous breakdown. She huffed and puffed and just went wild, calling me all sorts of names. She left the roof and I swear I could hear her shouting all the way down, "I hate Sarah, I hate Sarah, Hate, hate her!"

The next morning she told Mom that I was so mean to her that I caused her to break out in hives and she was never going back to Tar Beach! Mom was so annoyed with me, especially because I had a smile on my face that was just getting bigger and bigger. I was so happy that I thought I would bust!

"Sarah, what is wrong with you? Why do you always have to make her feel bad?" Mom asked.

It was no use explaining to Mom since she was always sticking up for Lila. I shrugged my shoulders and gave her my most innocent look, but it took only a second before I broke out laughing. "Mom, how many hives does Lila have? Is it really all over her face and body?" Mom stared at me and, for a minute, I thought for sure she was going to slap me but, instead, she walked out of the room, shaking her head. Meanwhile, I was feeling better and better by the second. I would never have to think about Lila coming up to Tar Beach again.

The other thing I love about Tar Beach is that I can read books up there that are taboo! Roxy's older sister Darlene is seventeen and very cool. She dates a lot of guys; one of them even goes to college. She knows a lot, and I mean a lot! She gives us tips on how to attract boys and other stuff, too.

Last summer she gave Roxy a copy of *Peyton Place,* and the two of us took turns reading chapters. Boy, we couldn't believe all the secrets and sex that went on in this pretty little picture perfect town. When we finished the book, we both agreed that you can't judge a book by its cover, and you sure as hell can never know what goes on behind closed doors.

The hot book this year is *Lolita.* When it came out, everyone was talking about it - Mom and her friends, girls at school, even Minnie and Selma. The one time I asked Mom about it, she told me that *Lolita* was not a book for me. "You have enough going on in your head. I don't want you should have the wrong ideas about things. Plenty time for you to read this later when you are older."

Now, I really wanted to read the book. I asked Darlene if she could get it, and, surprise, surprise, she already had a copy, read it, and loved it. "Don't tell Roxy, I gave this to you. I don't think she could take it, but you're different. There is something about you. Yeah, I think you can handle this one."

At first, I took what she said as a compliment, but, now, I'm not so sure. Anyway, now I have the book all to myself, I'm halfway finished, and I can see why everyone is so hush, hush over it. *Lolita* is the raunchiest book ever and I can't put it down! I can't say I understand it all. I mean, why does a twelve-year-old girl want to flirt with an old guy, like in his late thirties, with a name like Humbert Humbert, and he is her stepfather to boot? The idea of her wanting to have sex with him is totally perverted and creepy.

Hell, I'm a year older than Lolita, and, even though I imagine a lot of things, what's going on in her head is a stretch for me. Sometimes I'm scared for her, or should I be scared for Humbert? I'm all mixed up. Lolita makes me think about things that I don't want to think about or be reminded of. Like the other day, I got really bothered when I was reading about Lolita and Humbert actually having sex. I slammed the book shut and closed my eyes as tight as I could, hoping, that I could just tune out what I had read. But it was too late. My hand had already glided down to my thigh and found its way underneath my panties, where I was tingling and burning at the same time. I opened the book again and read the chapter over. Suddenly images of Lila lying next to me and our Friday night games came rushing back into my head.

My shame, my wetness, was already sliding down my leg. I threw the book to the ground. If I had a match, I'd burn it. Even though it was a summer afternoon, I started to shake like it was a cold winter's day. I looked around at the other rooftops. Could someone be out there watching me? But there was no one, just me with my guilt.

That night I couldn't sleep. I kept thinking about what Darlene had said when she gave me *Lolita* and then about what happened that afternoon. Maybe I am different from the other girls . . . but maybe not that different from Lolita and Lila.

Michael

Sarah's Surprise

It's been a few weeks since Sarah gallantly came to my rescue at the park. Boy, I will never forget Howie's face as she threatened him with ratting on him to his mother. If he could have hidden under a rock, he would have.

Sarah calls me her "all-time best friend!" I call her "my one and only" because she is the only friend I've ever had. Since I've met her, I actually am having fun. Sarah is funny, smart, and curious about everything, and I love the way she talks, with her hands flying all over the place, her laugh loud and contagious. I never know what she is going to say. Every day with Sarah is a surprise, like yesterday.

"Michael, what are you doing after your music lesson tomorrow?"

"Nothing. My lesson's been canceled. One of Maestro's daughters has a birthday and he has to help the Signora with the party. Why?"

Sarah claps her hands in excitement. "Goody. Ok, listen to me. Tomorrow morning be at my apartment at ten o' clock sharp. And you have to dress like we're going to the beach, all right?"

I know tomorrow is supposed to be really hot, high 90s, a

heat wave for the month of October. Who knows, maybe Mrs. Lanin will be driving us to the beach. No, she can't because she doesn't have a license yet or a car. Maybe Mr. Dudley will be driving us. That would be fun. I've never met anyone like him. Anyway, Sarah is pretty good at pretending, so I am sure whatever she has in store for me is going to be fun.

"Dress like you're going to the beach," she had said. I look into my closet and see right away I'm in trouble. There is nothing here that comes even close to something that I could wear for the beach. Nothing! I have no shorts, bathing suit, sneakers, and why would I? My parents have never taken me to the beach. I know Mother would like to go but Father does not believe in such outings. He thinks that if you have free time, you should do something constructive.

"If you want to find your place in life and be successful, you must study and practice. For you, Michael, music is your life, and it needs all of your attention!"

I love playing the violin but I want to do so much more. Last year I started to draw in secret. I have a few sketchbooks which I hide under my bed and in my closet. I can't let Father see them because he would not approve. I draw all kinds of things - trees, shapes, people I see on the street. But what I like to do most is portraits. I have one of the Maestro, the Signora, a few of Sarah that I'm working on, and one of Mother. I also started one of Tommy DeMarco, but it's hard. There's something about his eyes that I can't seem to get right. I noticed it the first day I saw him in front of his father's store and then again in the park that day with Sarah. His eyes kind of look right through you. I think about doing some more work on the portrait, when there is a soft knock on my door.

"Michael, your breakfast is ready," whispers Mother. "Make sure you eat. I am tired and going back to bed. Have a good day with your friend Sarah. I love you."

I look at my watch; it's nine o' clock. I have to get dressed but in what? I grab a white shirt from my closet, put it on, roll up the sleeves. Next my pants, roll up the cuffs. Once I put on my heavy shoes, I'm going to look pretty stupid. I unroll everything.

When I walk into the kitchen, I stare at my breakfast on the table - one plate, one fork, one glass of milk. Sometimes I get the feeling I'm the only one living here. I turn my back on the empty kitchen and tiptoe out of the apartment. Since it is Saturday morning, Father sleeps late. If I wake him, he will want to know where I am going and why. Father doesn't know about Sarah. Mother thought it would be best to keep her a secret.

By 9:45 a.m. I am standing in front of Sarah's door. I will wait till exactly 10 before I ring the doorbell. Even though Mr. and Mrs. Lanin are nothing like my parents, I don't want to barge in before I am expected. Father has always made a point of being promptly on time, not one minute before and not one minute after. I lean against the wall and wait. It takes only a second before the door opens and Sarah is standing in front of me.

"I thought I heard you breathing! Ok, now I want you to do what I say and don't ask any questions, got it?"

Before I can say a word, she turns me around and she blindfolds me and whispers in my ear. "Take my hand and follow me. We're going to take the stairs, this way no one can see us," she says, mysteriously.

We walk up three flights, take a right and walk up another set of narrow steps and stop. Sarah grunts as she opens what sounds like a heavy door. Instantly, a blast of heat swallows me. With her hand on my shoulders now, we take a few more steps and Sarah removes the blindfold. She twirls me around and points.

"What do you think?"

"I . . . think . . . it's fantastic!"

"It is, isn't it? Welcome to Tar Beach!"

Sarah has taken the tar rooftop and turned it into a beach, of course without the water and sand. But everything else is perfect. There are two yellow and blue beach chairs with blue beach towels draped over them. A low, white plastic folding table sits on a multi-colored striped blanket. On top of the table, there is a pitcher with lemons painted on it, yellow paper cups, a bag of potato chips, a small bottle with dark, thick purple liquid in it, Sarah's transistor radio and a large yellow straw bag. I'm taking it all in when Sarah starts to laugh at me.

"What's funny?" I ask.

Remember, I said, "Beach?"

"Sarah, I don't have any clothes like that. I'm sorry." I turn my face away because I am so embarrassed.

"Well, we have to do something about what you're wearing because otherwise you're going to roast up here and that won't be fun. Here, sit down. First things first . . . take off your shoes and socks, then roll up your pants." I do as she says. "Now, your shirt."

I feel awkward. I've never done anything like this before. While Sarah is giving me orders, she steps out of her shorts, takes her blouse off, and in seconds, she's standing before me in a bright yellow ruffled bathing suit. I start to blush.

"Oh, Michael, don't be so nervous . . . it's not like we're naked."

Sarah sits down, gets busy pouring lemonade into two cups, finds the rock and roll station on her radio, and opens up the chips. Everything seems so natural to her.

"Michael, are you going to just stand there all day?"

I take my clothes and put them in a neat pile and tuck them under my chair. It feels so unfamiliar to be exposed like this, with a girl, on a rooftop, pretending to be on a beach ... but it feels good, and that happens a lot when I am with Sarah. I stand there waiting for her to tell me what to do next.

"Come close . . . I want to put some of my special suntan oil on you. I make this myself. A few drops of iodine, olive oil, and grape juice! You'll see. At the end of day you will be so tan and gorgeous, everyone will think you are a movie star!"

Sarah opens the bottle of oil and pours a few drops into her hands. She moves behind me and, with smooth strokes, she applies the oil on to my back. When she is done, she turns me around and does my chest. Even though I'm sweating from the hot sun, the sensation of someone other than my mother touching me sends a shiver right through me.

"Now, you can do me."

The suntan oil feels thick and greasy in my hands. Sarah can tell that I'm uncomfortable. She takes both of my hands and rests them on her shoulders. "Michael, I'm not asking you to massage my chest, just my back and shoulders. Just do as I did to you, all right?"

I rub her down, slowly and carefully. When I'm done, Sarah tells me to sit down in the beach chair. She digs into her beach bag, takes out a pair of large pink and yellow sunglasses, and puts them on; she flips her hair in the air, sits down, and crosses her legs.

"You like?" she asks as she winks at me.

When she flirts like this, I am always at a loss for words. She goes back into her bag and comes out with another pair of sunglasses, framed in blue. She leans over and puts them on me. "There you go. I didn't want you to get jealous. Now we can both look fabulous!"

Sarah turns up the radio and takes my hand. A song plays, the music and lyrics are so beautiful that I get lost in it and find myself practically in tears. When it's over, Sarah is staring at me with complete surprise.

"Michael Stein, I think I will love you forever!"

The rest of the afternoon we laugh and sing. I dance clumsily to songs I have never heard before and we talk about our dreams. Sarah wants to be a famous actress and to apply to Performing Arts; I want to be a famous musician and artist and will be applying to Music and Art. We have so many things in common. Everything is as perfect as it can be. I am happier than I have ever been.

I think we fell asleep for a while because Sarah is tapping me on my knee "Michael, you're not going to believe this!"

Sarah has a mirror pointed at my face. I stare at my image and panic rises in my throat. I jump up from the chair and frantically try to wipe the oil off my chest and face but except for beads of sweat, all the oil has been absorbed into my skin.

"Michael, what the hell are you doing?"

"Sarah, when my father sees me this way . . . he is going to kill me!"

I keep rubbing my body as if I have hundreds of ants crawling over me. Sarah grabs my hands and forces them down against my thighs. She holds on to them until I stop shaking and then sits me down in the chair.

"Michael, talk to me."

How can I explain to her about Father - that I can't tell him about Tar Beach, that she is a secret, that I can't tell him that, since meeting her I feel normal for the first time?

"Aren't you exaggerating a little? I mean, what's the big deal? How angry can he get? And like, what's the worst thing that can happen? He grounds you, makes you practice 100 hours more than you already do? Besides your mother won't let him hurt you . . . right? Gee, all you did was be with me, listen to some music, have fun, and get a tan."

"Father doesn't know about you, and if he met you, he wouldn't like you at all . . . and he doesn't believe in fun!"

"You can't be serious! I know that, when your father meets me, he will love me." Sarah smiles. "After all, I'm adorable."

"Sarah, I can't explain it, but my parents are different, especially Father. Maybe they were other people in Germany before they had me. Maybe I changed everything. I don't know. But the one thing I can be sure of is that, when he sees me, he will punish me."

Sarah stops laughing. She is staring at me with such sadness that I feel sick. I have to leave. I stand up, and right away the knot in my stomach rises and . . . I throw up all over Sarah's pretty blue blanket.

Sarah quickly wipes my mouth with one of her towels and then, as if I am a small child, she puts my shirt back on, buttons it, unrolls my pants, puts my socks on, and helps me with my shoes. Then she does something that will stay with me forever. She holds me in her arms and rocks me like a baby—and we both cry.

Lila

The Unspoken Rule

I had just finished brushing my hair when she came up behind me and grabbed the brush from my hand. I must have turned too quickly because the handle of the brush hit my forehead, where a telltale bump would soon appear. That would not be a good thing. The unspoken rule was that my face was out of bounds. Mom got so mad at her clumsiness and carelessness that she had to hurt me more. This time she took the hairbrush and ran it across my arm back and forth, leaving bright red marks. I was so afraid that she was going to take my skin off that I screamed out in pain. That's when the door opened and Daddy walked in.

He was supposed to be working overtime and not expected home till late tonight. I don't know which of us was more surprised. Mom always planned her attacks on me when there was no chance of Daddy learning about it. But today she picked the wrong time. The three of us kind of stood frozen, unable to move. I wanted to run into Daddy's arms, but I saw his hand, fingers go stiff, stretched out and aimed for Mom's chest. He pushed her against the wall with such force that she slid down like a broken doll.

"Fritzy, you do not move," he said in a voice so cold that I felt as if a wall of ice had fallen and shattered before me. Then

Daddy put his arms around my waist and led me out.

Daddy took me to Hannah's where I sat on the couch while he spoke to her in whispers; then he left to deal with Mom. When Sarah came home, she wasn't too happy to see me and ran out as quickly as she had come in. Hannah called after her, but Sarah did not come back till much later. I was OK with that because I had Hannah all to myself.

Sarah

Michael Leaves Tar Beach

I beg Michael to talk to my mom. She can make anyone feel better, and I'm sure if she talks to his mom, they can work things out. But he isn't having any of it. "Sarah, your mom can't help me. I'm sorry I scared you. Thank you for bringing me to Tar Beach. Don't worry about me, I'll be OK."

I don't believe him for a minute. No one can go that bonkers and then say he's OK. I walk him downstairs and watch him as he goes across to his side of the building. "Hey, can I call you later?" I shout out.

Michael stops for a second, looks at me, and shakes his head no. My heart sinks. I am staring at the saddest boy I've ever seen. I wave and he's gone.

I have to tell Mom. I know she's not going to be happy about this. She warned me to be careful, that the Steins were different, but Michael needs to have someone stick up for him. And that has to be me because who else is there? I'm his only friend. Besides, it's just not right for a kid to be that scared of a parent. No way.

I should go back up to Tar Beach to pack up and put everything away, but it can wait. Right now the important thing is to speak to Mom. If anyone can fix things, it's her. I run up the steps and am out of breath when I get to my floor. Whew, I have to sit, take a second. I plop down on the steps and think about what I'm going to say to Mom. I can't sound hysterical.

I go over everything that happened today, when I hear voices. I jump up and step into the middle of the hallway. I look around, but everything goes quiet. I recognize Fritzy's voice right away - she's crying. I stand back against the wall and inch my way closer to the Rosen apartment. Max is shouting. His angry footsteps are pounding the floor, back and forth. I move a little closer to their door - there's a crash! Fritzy cries out like a sick cat. "No Max, no more, I am sorry. I did not mean what I said! Please."

She's pleading with him. What's he doing to her? Then there's another crash. Oh no, he's walking towards the door, he's unlocking it. Shit, I've got to get out of here. If he finds me here, he'll know I've been eavesdropping. Crap, the door is opening. I turn around quickly. My apartment is down the hall but I don't think I can make it. Instead, I hurry up the steps and hide on the next floor landing. From here I can see the Rosen's door.

Max comes out of the apartment. He looks like he's going to leave but then he stops. He puts his face in his hands and rubs his forehead. From where I am, I can't see his face all that good, but I'm betting he looks terrible. He moves his hands down to his side and clenches his fists. He's standing still. The hallway is spooky quiet. Then, Max turns back to the door and starts to bang his head, one . . . two . . . three . . . four times against the door. He's muttering to himself but I can't make out what he's saying. What's he going to do next? Geez, I have to pee. I squeeze as tight as I can. I'll have to hold it in till he makes his next move. Oh, I wish he'd leave or go back into the apartment. Wait, he's taking something out of his pocket . . . looks like a handkerchief. He's wrapping it around one of his hands. He mutters something again and then finally he walks down the steps. Only when I hear the front door to the building close, do I move.

I jump down the steps to my floor and run as fast as I can to my apartment, praying that Mom is home. As soon as I'm in, I lock the door and shout out, "Mom!"

"I'm right here, sweetheart."

Right in front of me, in the living room, Mom is sitting on the couch, holding Lila in her arms. It's the last thing I expected or wanted to see! "What is she doing here?"

"Lila's been hurt."

Mom gently parts the hair over Lila's eyes. There is a big ugly bump on her forehead. I look her up and down and see deep red scratches on her arm. Then I realize that's what Fritzy and Max were fighting about. It was Fritzy who did this to her. For a second, I feel sorry for her.

"Sarah, I have asked Lila to stay here tonight. She will sleep on the couch. We will make her comfortable, right, sweetheart?"

No, it is not all right? Why can't Mom see how unhappy I am—is she blind?

Right now, this very minute, I feel angry, confused, and more alone than I have ever felt in my life. I have nowhere to go except back up to Tar Beach.

Michael

Late Afternoon

Standing in front of the mirror, I stare at my sunburned face. There is no way for me to hide the way I look. Father is going to see me. He will hit me right away, or he will stand there in total silence, waiting for me to give him an explanation. And, all the while, he is going to be thinking about how he is going to punish me. I have no idea what to tell him. If I lie, make something up, and he finds out, it will only make everything worse. I don't know what to do. I have to talk to Mother. I go to her bedroom and knock gently on her door.

"Mother, are you awake? I need to talk to you, please."

"Come in, Michael," she says in a voice so soft, I can hardly hear her.

I open the door and, like always, I am surprised at how dark and quiet it is in here. It's as if nothing else exists outside of this room. But it does - I exist, Father exists, and, in a few hours, he will be home, and I cannot stop shaking at the thought of it.

I pull the shades up halfway so she is not blinded by the sunlight, turn the bed lamp on, and sit down at the edge of her bed. I look around the room. It's three o'clock in the afternoon, and she has been here all day, sleeping, trying not to remember the things that always make her so sad, things I know so little about. By her side are two open photo albums. Sometimes Mother lets me sit with her and she tells me about each of the photographs. Most of them are of Mother and Father in Germany, at another time, before me, when they were young, when they were other people. Mother sits up, brushes her hand over my face, and stares at me in surprise.

"Michael, where have you been?"

"I went to Tar Beach with Sarah. It's the rooftop in her building. She has a pretend beach up there."

"A beach, on the roof? What a lovely imagination your Sarah has," my mother says with delight.

"It was wonderful. I was having such a good time that I didn't realize how burnt I got. What do I tell Father? I don't want him to know about Sarah. He'll make me stop seeing her. I don't want to do that."

"There is no doubt that your father will be upset. Why don't you go and wash up and change into clean clothes - you smell of oil. Give me a little time to think." She starts to giggle.

"Mother," I say in a panic. She starts to giggle more. Here I am desperate and she is giggling!

"Oh, Michael, please forgive me, but right now you remind me of the first summer your father and I spent together. In those days he was a very different man. There was a wonderful beach not too far from the center of Berlin, where we lived, called the *Strandbad Wannsee*. We rode our bikes out there on summer weekends. So much fun we had in those days, swimming, lying in the sun. It was quite wonderful."

Mother picks up one of the albums and starts to turn the pages, looking for a particular photograph. I know which one. I have seen it before. It is of the two of them sitting side by side on a rock, their faces turned to each other, the sea behind them. And they are kissing.

"See how tan he is, just like you. Poor man, he always ended up with a sunburn, just like you now. I wonder, when he comes home, if he will have the same memory as I and if he will be able to see how much you look like him. Probably not. Oh, well, we will find out soon." Then she starts to giggle again, like a little girl.

This is crazy. What's wrong with her? Why isn't she as scared as I am?"

"Mother, are you all right?"

Her face, which was so happy just seconds ago, turns suddenly into a mask of sorrow. The change is so quick and overwhelming that I can't help but cry.

"My poor baby, look at you. What have I done to you?"

Mother shakes her head and puts both my hands in hers and caresses them. "Michael, I want you to go to your room, read, or, even better, take a nap if you can."

"But, Mother?"

"Listen to me. As it happens, your father called this morning from work to tell me that he has gotten a big promotion. He is now foreman of the department. Maybe today is the day to make changes. Let us see."

"Are you going to tell him about Sarah?"

"Yes, I think I will and some other things too. Do not worry."

I hope she is right. Maybe today my father will be different and everything will be OK. I wish, hope and . . . pray that it will be.

I fall asleep and, when I wake up, the room is dark. There is the smell of something roasting coming from the kitchen. I look out my window to see if Sarah is in her bedroom, but her shade is down and her light is not on. I feel bad leaving her like I did today. But there wasn't anything she could do.

Mother knocks softly on my door and comes into my room. She puts on the light and stands in the doorway, dressed in a pretty blue and white flowered dress. Her long wavy hair is loose on her shoulders and she looks beautiful. She twirls around and curtsies.

"So what do you think of your mother? Not bad, right?"

I have to be dreaming. None of this seems real or is this real and everything else has been a dream? All I know is that nothing is the same since I got home this afternoon.

"Listen. Your father will be home soon. Do not come into the kitchen till I call you, OK, my love?"

When she leaves, I realize that I have never seen my mother this way. I know what I need to do. I kneel down and pull out my sketch pad and box of pencils from underneath my bed. I sit on the floor and start to draw. My hands move as if they have a mind of their own. I don't ever want to forget seeing her like I just did, standing in the doorway, smiling, happy, in her pretty blue and white flowered dress.

Sarah

Back To Tar Beach

I've been up here a while, thinking all sorts of crazy things. Like, what if Michael's father does hurt him? What if his mother can't protect him? All these crazy thoughts are giving me a terrible headache. I've bitten my nails down so low that they're bleeding. Crap! And now it's getting dark and neither Mom or Dad has come looking for me. Do they even know how long I have been gone? Do they care? Probably not, because they're too busy taking care of poor Lila.

The skin on my arms is itching. Geez, I'm getting red bumps all over, just like Lila. Oh, my God, do I have eczema too? Is it catching? I have to go home. I need a bath filled with ice to stop me from scratching.

As soon as I walk into the apartment I hear Mom, Dad, and Lila in the kitchen, talking away, laughing, just like a big, happy family. I put my hands over my ears and go into my room. I am so tired. I don't have the energy to take a bath. I just want to lie down, shut out the world, and go to sleep. After an hour of tossing and turning, I get up and sit by my window and look out at Michael's. His shade is down, the room is dark. I open the window and lean out as far as I can, hoping to hear his violin, but there is nothing.

Then the worst possible thought pops into my head. What if his father killed him? I run into the living room . . . I need Mom . . . I'm really scared, but all the lights are out, even the ones in their bedroom. Everyone is asleep, including Lila on the couch. I go back to my room and sit at the window, where I will wait till Michael pulls up his shade and smiles at me. Please, God, let him be OK. I will do anything, even be nicer to Lila—I promise!

Michael

Mother Stands Up To Father

Mother calls from the kitchen, "Michael, your Father is home."

I look at my watch. It's six o' clock. I've lost track of time. I've been sitting here, drawing for hours. There are several of Tar Beach with the beach chairs, some of Sarah posing for me with her sunglasses, the rooftops of the other buildings, the sun beating down on them.

I put them away in a box where I keep my drawings and slide it under my bed. Then I check underneath my mattress and pull out my new drawing pad. I lift the cover and, with my finger, I trace the outline of Tommy Demarco's face. It's not as good as I would like it to be, but it doesn't matter. I would never show it to him anyway. Besides, I can't imagine what his reaction would be.

"Michael, please come in now, supper is ready," Mother calls out sweetly.

I tuck the pad underneath my mattress, right in the middle. I can't have Father find any of my drawings - especially not the one of Tommy. I shoot a quick look into my bedroom mirror and see that my sunburn hasn't faded. If anything, I look worse. My face is red and small blisters are bubbling on my forehead. Well, it's too late now. Maybe Father's promotion will make him less angry.

I walk into the kitchen and the smell of roasted meat cooking in vinegar and spices fill my nostrils. The everyday plastic kitchen tablecloth printed with green and red apples has been replaced with a white lace one. There is a vase with fresh flowers and a crystal decanter with red wine.

Mother is standing at the table. She looks up at me and gives me a wink. Father is in the doorway. He looks as surprised as me.

"Judith, what is all this?"

I can't tell if he is pleased or annoyed.

"I thought it would be nice to celebrate your good news," Mother says, with a sunny smile.

"Yes, yes, well, it is about time my superiors start to recognize my intelligence. However, I still have to get them to realize that I am more than just a typesetter or foreman. I am a writer, a journalist. That is what I did in Germany and that is what I should be doing here! But you know how those . . ." Mother interrupts him before he goes on to his usual complaints.

"In time, Joseph, you'll see, you will get what you deserve. But for tonight, instead of getting yourself all upset, let us all sit, make a toast, laugh, and be happy. We have not done this in a while."

Mother pours some wine for herself and Father and then a little for me. She raises her glass.

"To you, Joseph, congratulations!"

Father looks so confused that he is speechless. He has not taken his eyes off the table or Mother since he has come into the kitchen. He sips his wine and his face softens a little. Is it possible that he's going to give in to Mother's efforts to celebrate?

"This is nice, yes, very nice; thank you, the both of you."

Father directs his attention to me and looks at me for the first time since he has walked into the kitchen. His face turns into shock, his eyes are practically bulging!

"WHAT! Your face! What is wrong with your face?"

Mother quickly comes to the rescue.

"Well, he doesn't look as handsome as usual, actually he

looks awful." Mother puts her hand to her mouth, trying to control her laughter.

"Michael has gotten a sunburn, Joseph, and you know what is funny is that, when he came home today, he reminded me so much of you when we used to spend our days at the beach and you, too, would get too much sun. Oh my, how you would carry on!" Mother is now laughing so hard, she is holding on to her stomach. I have never seen her this way.

"Judith, shut up! Michael, explain yourself!"

The tone of his voice makes me stand to attention. I'm in for it no matter what. I have to tell him the truth. If I lie, it will just make things worse.

"I . . . have a friend, her name is Sarah. She is in my grade at school and she lives right next door. Today, she invited me to Tar Beach, that's her rooftop and we . . . "

Father glares at me and then at Mother and roars, "What is this nonsense? Tar Beach? Sarah? Really, Judith, can't you watch over your son or were you in bed all day . . . again? Can't I trust you to do one thing right? How many times do I have to tell the both of you not to mix with anyone from here?"

Mother ignores Father and takes her wine and drinks it all down in one gulp. Father's chest swells up; I think any minute smoke will flare out of his mouth and nostrils.

"Mother didn't know," I blurt out. "It isn't her fault. I lied to her, told her I was going to the library. Please, I just wanted to have some fun . . . Sarah is my first friend." Tears start to fill my eyes.

"Michael, it is bad enough that you lied and disobeyed me, but I will not have you stand before me and behave like a crybaby."

Father gets up and walks towards me. He is about to unbuckle his belt, when suddenly Mother sweeps her arm across the table, sending the dishes, silverware, flowers, decanter, flying to the floor! Father looks down. There is a pool of red wine spreading over the white tablecloth, drops falling onto the white and green linoleum floor. The flowers are crushed. My God, what is he going to do?

For the second time this night, Father is again speechless. I can see his mind working, trying to understand everything that is happening. The expression on his face turns to rage as he sees Mother's face light up with excitement.

"You know what Michael? I do not feel like having supper tonight, and, apparently, Joseph, you do not either and, since you never want to do anything that is fun and at the spur of the moment, I am taking Michael out for a banana split!"

Mother pulls me up from my chair and leads me out of the kitchen. As we leave the apartment, she turns around and, in a singsong voice, calls out to father.

"Joseph, please do not wait up for us!"

Afraid that Father is going to try to stop us, I turn and take a quick glance back at him. He is staring at the kitchen floor, his fist tapping the table in slow deliberate beats. His body looks as if it has turned to stone.

We're four blocks away from our building, but I'm still looking back to see if father is following us.

"He's not coming Michael," says Mother. "As a matter of fact, I would not be surprised if, when we got home, he will be sitting right where we left him. Tonight was a shock for him. He's not used to me standing up to him. Now, how would you like to go shopping?"

"Where and for what, I ask?"

"For you silly, you need some new clothes. If we hurry, we can make it to Schuler's Men's store before it closes. Then we can go for ice cream, as promised."

For the last few months, Mother hasn't moved faster than a snail. Now she grabs my hand and we start to run. We run so fast that, before I know it, we're standing in front of the store. There is a sign on the front door, "Open nine to seven." We both look at my watch. Mother smiles.

"Wonderful, we have fifteen minutes till it closes!"

We enter the store making a grand entrance with our laughter. Flush and out of breath, Mother leads me up and down the aisles, looking at everything. We come to a full halt when we get to a table with a stack of boys' dungarees piled on top of it.

"Hmm," Mothers says, sounding confused. "There are so many to choose from. You know, Michael, I'm not even sure what size you are."

"Don't worry, I know."

"Thank goodness, otherwise we might be here forever. OK, go and pick out a pair. Then I think we should get you some new summer shirts and how about a pair of those, what do they call them, the ones that all the boys are wearing?"

Before I can answer her, a salesman appears at the other side of the table. The name tag on the lapel of his suit jacket reads "Marvin."

"Excuse me; I was just getting ready to close. Is there anything I can help you with?" he asks politely.

Mother puts on her best smile and introduces the two of us. Within seconds, she has him eating out of her hand. I'm guessing that Marvin is probably willing to keep the store open for as long as Mother wants.

One hour later, we leave with a large shopping bag with new socks, a pair of dungarees, T-shirts, a pair of black Keds with white soles, and a red bathing suit. As we walk away, Marvin stands in front of the glass doors of the store. He waves good-bye to us. Mother then turns around and does something so unexpected that I think my eyes are going to pop out of my head—Mother blows Marvin a kiss! Even though it's dark now, I can see Marvin blushing. Mother continues to keep blowing kisses at him till we turn the corner.

"Michael, you swear you will not tell anyone what a flirt I was tonight. Promise me?" she says with a teasing smile. OK, now let's go have that ice-cream."

I pinch myself to make sure everything that has happened is real. Suddenly I think of Sarah and wonder if she'll ever want to talk to me again. If not, I can't blame her. Tomorrow, first thing, I'll go to her apartment and ask her to forgive me.

There aren't any customers at Harry's so we have the place to ourselves. We order our banana splits with everything on them and two Cokes. While we wait, Mother announces that things are going to be different from now on. She's talking a mile a minute, when the front door opens. I don't turn around to see who it is, but Mother goes very quiet and her eyes glance over my head. She seems to drift away, staring at whoever has walked in. I go on eating but I'm also praying that it's not Father. Please don't let it be him, please!

I slowly turn my head and look. A man sits down at the counter. It's Mr. Rosen, Lila's father.

"Mother, do you know him?"

"No, but I have seen him in the neighborhood. He always walks with this beautiful girl. I assume it is his daughter. They seem happy, close . . . and now he is sitting there by himself, looking so very sad. He reminds me of . . . me."

It's midnight and I am wide awake. I just keep going over all the wonderful things that happened today and this evening. A glass of milk and some cookies are what I need. I walk towards the kitchen, trying to be quiet, when I hear something that just seems so out of place. I turn to my parents bedroom and listen . . . I can't believe it! No! They can't be! I feel sick. I run back to my room and put a pillow over my head and ears to block out the noise of my parents making love.

Sarah

The Next Morning

"Good morning, sleepy head," Mom says to me, too sweetly. "I never thought you would get up."

"I'm lucky I got any sleep, period! What with Lila moaning on the couch all night. But I guess you knew that because you probably spent the whole night with her."

"*Gotteniu*, Sarah, please don't start this morning. There are times when you just have to bend a little, and, if you can't, better you should say nothing."

"Well, I'll be quiet then, but I'll be much nicer when she goes back to her own apartment and sleeps there!"

"That is too bad because Lila is not going home so quickly. Max and I think it would be better for her to stay here for a few days. Max and Fritzy have to work some things out. And I want to make her feel safe and comfortable. So I would like Lila to sleep in your room. I'll make up a small bed for her, better than the couch. You are a good girl, Sarah, so I am asking you, begging you, for this one time only, let it be."

I could not believe what Mom was asking of me. Has she ever listened to me at all . . . about anything I have ever said, anything? I walk out of the kitchen, not saying a word. I get dressed as quickly as I can and leave. Not sure where I'm going, but I do not want to see Lila this morning. Let her have the pancakes.

I take a bus to the Grand Concourse and walk around, killing time at Alexander's Department Store, till the movie theater opens up. I can sit here and watch at least two movies. The later I get home the better.

It's dark by the time I come home. I hear the three of them in the kitchen eating supper. I walk straight into my bedroom. I guess Mom is finally realizing how angry I am because she and Dad don't even call out my name, ask me to come in, or anything.

As soon as I enter my bedroom, I see the cot made up in the corner of the room. Mom made it look pretty, with new flowered sheets and one of her quilts. Folded at the end of the bed is one of my nightgowns.

Unbelievable! The whole business is making me so very tired, I collapse on my bed and close my eyes. I don't know how long I was out but, when I wake up, Lila is lying next to me, her face so close to mine that I can smell her breath. She's smiling at me.

"Lila, get the hell off of my bed!" Unfazed, she doesn't move an inch.

"How come you didn't have supper with us? Your mom is such a great cook."

I lose it, that's it! I jump out of bed and push her off and she falls to the floor. "There is no way you are sleeping in my bed, with me! No way! Do you hear me?" She picks herself up and sits back down on the bed.

"Oh come on, Sarah, I thought it would be fun, just like when we were little."

"It was never fun, Lila." I point to the cot. "That's where you sleep." I push her again but this time harder.

"I am going to tell your mother you hit me."

"No, you won't Lila, because if you do, I'll tell everyone at school that your mother beats you up all the time and that you're really an orphan and that you have horrible nasty scabs all over your body."

I don't know where I came up with the orphan bit but, between that and the scabs, my threats knocked her for a loop. For a second I swear she is going to come at me but, instead, she lies down on the cot, takes the quilt, and covers herself up to her chin, her eyes glaring at me with pure hatred.

I turn off the lights and roll over on my side with my back facing her. I have never stood up to Lila like this. I know that Lila will not let me forget. Not sure how or when, but she will do something to pay me back.

Lila

Wishing It Could Be Different

I've been watching Sarah sleep and thinking about all the mean things she said to me tonight. Her words really got to me, making me feel tired of being me and reminding me of how lonely I really am. Right now it would be so nice if I could sleep next to her in the same bed and feel the warmth of her body, just two girlfriends who look out for each other, someone to talk to, someone to trust. But that will never happen. It's too late, there's too much stuff between us.

I wish we could start all over again, right from the beginning, except that's stupid because, for everything to be different, I'd have to have another mother. Daddy says if there hadn't been a war, he never would have married her. He promises to tell me the story one day but, right now, this minute, I don't care. I just wish I had never been born.

Michael

One Week Later

I'm hoping that when Sarah sees me this morning, she'll forgive me. I know it wasn't right for me not to call, to disappear like I did after my panic attack on Tar Beach. I wanted to tell her everything that happened that night when Mother stood up to Father. How wonderful it felt to be free of him. It was as if we didn't have a care in the world. But, then, hearing the two of them later, in their bedroom, I felt as if Mother had betrayed me. All night I had been riding high until that moment. It was as if I had been flying from the minute we left Father and went on our shopping spree, seeing Mother happy and laughing, feeling like I was being held up by hundreds of balloons, and then they popped, plunging me back to reality.

The next morning I pretended to be sick. I guess I'm a pretty good actor because Mother didn't give me a hard time about not going to school. I think she was actually happy to have me home to care for. It gave her the chance to show me how she was going to keep her promise. Father, on the other hand, didn't quite believe me but let Mother have her way. After two days, though, he wasn't as convinced as she was and suggested that I should consider going back to school. What surprised me was that he didn't scold me or order me, the way he usually would.

So here I am, in front of Sarah's door, one week later, all dressed in my new look. I even combed my hair differently. Instead of letting it fall, covering my eyes, to protect me from ever making eye contact with anyone, I combed it back, ready for me to see everyone.

Feeling nervous, I ring Sarah's doorbell. When she opens the door, her mouth drops open.

"I don't like the way you're staring at me. I look silly, right? Or worse, stupid?"

"Michael, it's not that. I just didn't expect to see you ever again, and here you are, looking so incredibly breathtaking, cooler than anyone I know, and you expect me to act like it's nothing. Michael Stein, you scared the shit out of me!"

"I'm sorry about spoiling your day at Tar Beach, about freaking out, about not calling you, about everything. It's just that it's complicated. You see, my father is very strict. There are rules that I have to live by, things I can and can't do. Tar Beach and having fun are two things he would not accept. It's hard to explain. And I was afraid of what my father was going to do to me, how he would decide to punish me."

Sarah bites her lips and looks deeply into my eyes. She moves closer to me and gives me a kiss that is loving and kind, I immediately feel safe, protected.

"Sarah, who's out there? What are you doing?" shouts Mrs. Lanin from inside.

Sarah turns and bobs her head around as if she's looking for something.

"Mom, it's nothing!" Sarah yells. "Michael, give me a few minutes and I'll meet you downstairs, OK?"

I don't have a chance to say anything because Sarah is pushing me down the stairs. A few minutes later, she comes down, acting as if someone is chasing her and forces me to run with her to the Deli. Once inside, she rushes me to a booth, where we plunk down and catch our breath. Before I can ask her why we were running away and from whom, she wags her finger in front of my face.

"Speak," she says in a commanding voice.

So I do. First I tell her about Mother's depression, how I miss her when she decides to shut out the world, including me. How she talked to Father that night, how she promised me that things were going to be different and what we did after. I even told her about seeing Mr. Rosen and how Mother reacted to him. When I finish, Sarah is sobbing like a baby.

"Michael, if I could, I would kidnap you and have you come and live with me and my parents for good, where we would love and protect you forever!"

My heart feels like it's going to burst. Mother may try her best, but I think it will be Sarah Lanin who changes my life.

Sarah

Beautiful Girls

When we say goodbye, Michael thanks me for listening. He says, "I've never told anybody about my parents. It felt good."

I run upstairs, excited to see Mom. I'm ready to forgive her and shower her with kisses. After listening to Michael talking about his mother and father and, knowing what I do about the Rosens, I realize that I'm pretty lucky to have the parents I have.

Mom can't help being as nice as she is to Lila and to everyone, for that matter. I should try to be more like her. It's kind of hard for me to hide my feelings about Lila in front of Mom. From now on I'm going to give it my best shot. And whatever has happened between Lila and me will just have to be between us.

As soon as I open the door, I hear their voices chatting away. Mom, Max, and Lila. I stand in the doorway to the kitchen and say hello. Max immediately gets up and takes my hands in his and kisses them.

"My dear, Sarah, Lila has told me how good you have been to her. Letting her share your bed was a very kind act. She also told me how she kept you up all this week by talking to you late in the night, what a good listener you were. It pleases me and your mother so much to see the two of you as close as you are - just like sisters. I thank you from the bottom of my heart."

Max is so sincere. I think he's going to cry. Lila comes up to me and puts her arm tightly around my waist. She smiles at me with one of her best sugar-coated expressions. I look at Mom and I swear she's about to cry. I'm surrounded by so much emotion that I realize I have no choice but to play this out. I hug Lila back and gaze at her, beaming with sisterly love.

Lila and I are so convincing that Mom spreads her arms out like an eagle, takes a giant breath, steps forward and presses our heads so deep into her chest that for a minute I think she's going to smother the both of us.

"My beautiful girls, how it makes my heart full to see the two of you like this. I know sometimes you have little disagreements, but, when it matters, you are there for each other. This is what is important! This is what counts!"

Wrong, Mom, I want to say. What's important is that Lila knows now I'm no longer afraid of her. She's no longer in charge.

November

Michael

Lila Waits For Him

OK, this is weird. Lila is standing right outside of Maestro's building. I've never seen her in this part of the neighborhood before. It's like ten blocks away from where we live.

"Hi, Lila, what are you doing here?"

"Thought I'd surprise you and walk home with you," Lila says, like it's an ordinary thing to do.

This is more than weird - it's trouble. Walk me home? It's not like we're friends or anything. Sarah works hard at keeping us as far away from each other as possible. I've never even spoken to her for longer than a few minutes. If Sarah catches me with Lila, she'll kill me.

"Oh, Michael, don't be so nervous, relax. My father found a singing coach for me. And, she just happens to live in that building across the street from this one. I saw you walk in before with your violin. I asked my coach if she knew any music teachers here. It just so happens she is a friend of your Maestro. I love the sound of that name, so romantic. So isn't this a great coincidence?"

I don't want to tell her what I'm really thinking. Better to say nothing.

"Anyway, now we can walk home together and get to know

each other. I know you're like Sarah's private property and all that, but she doesn't have to know about this. It will be our secret," Lila says, as she winks at me.

Lila laughs. Maybe it's because I'm nervous, but I start to laugh, too. The difference is that her laugh sounds for real and mine sounds like I'm gurgling water after brushing my teeth. Talk about feeling like a jerk! The thing is that Lila's laugh is a nice one, and she doesn't sound mean or anything.

We walk home and talk about all sorts of things. Lila heard I was trying out for Music and Art and thinks it's exciting. She's trying out for the Performing Arts Dance Department. Her father's hoping that taking voice lessons will give her an even better chance of getting in. While I listen to her, I'm thinking that once Sarah hears this, she's going to freak out. Sarah is also trying out for Performing Arts but for the Drama Department. If, for some reason, she doesn't get in and Lila does, oh my God, I can't imagine how that will make Sarah feel.

We're finally home and standing in front of Lila's building. I should say a quick goodbye, just in case Sarah is around. "Ok, here we are. Thanks for walking me home," I say, trying to sound sincere and not anxious.

"Yeah, it was cool! We should do this every week. Now I see why Sarah likes you so much. You're so easy to talk to."

Then out of nowhere, Lila throws her arms around my neck. She gets all snugly like, rests her head on my shoulder, playfully blows in my ear, and whispers to me. "You know, Michael, I'm much nicer than Sarah, and I know things."

Know things? What's she talking about? And do I want to know?

Droplets of perspiration dribble down my forehead. But it doesn't seem to bother Lila. She holds on to me even tighter. I try to pull away as politely as I can. At the same time, I'm trying to not look her in the eye, I hear voices. Lila and I both turn around and my stomach sinks to the floor. It's Sarah and her Mother. They're walking up the block towards us, carrying shopping bags. As soon as Sarah spots us, she drops her shopping bag. Groceries are spilling out onto the street.

"Oh no," I say out loud.

"Sarah, what in the world?" says her mother.

I try to break away from Lila, but she won't let me go. She grabs my hand and pulls me back to her. I shake her off and run to scoop up the groceries rolling around on the sidewalk.

"Traitor!" Sarah shouts.

I look up at Sarah. She's got a finger in each ear so she can't hear me. Her eyes are closed shut, her lips squeezed together. There's no mistaking what she's thinking. I've been caught in an act of treason, punishable only by death.

Sarah

Freaking Out

"I have invited the Rosens for Thanksgiving," Mom announces.

"What the hell, Mom, you can't be serious!" I shout in disbelief.

People at the supermarket start to stare at me. Mom pulls me to the side.

"Watch your tongue, Sarah, and lower your voice. The Rosens don't have anywhere to go. I feel bad for Lila and Max. Minnie and Selma are coming, too, and they will make sure Fritzy behaves herself, and I expect you to do the same. Besides, its only one day a year. I am sure you can handle it."

What I can handle and what I want to do are two different things. I'm so angry at Mom that I don't say a word to her all the way home. Once we turn the corner onto our block I go into shock!

The shopping bag I'm holding drops out of my hands, groceries bounce all over the sidewalk. But I don't care, because down the block in front of my building are Michael and Lila. She has her arms wrapped around Michael's neck, her head on his shoulder. I feel sick and furious at the same time. I want to kill her! I stare at Michael and try not to break down. Instead, I breathe and go for the attack.

"Traitor!" I shout at him. How could you?"

"Sarah, for God's sake!" yells Mom. "Help me!"

Michaels's eyes are darting from mine to Mom's. He's in a panic about what to do.

Mom calls out his name and asks him to help. Lila comes forward and shoves Michael towards the spilled groceries. She, Michael, and Mom run around like the Three Stooges, scooping up boxes, cookies, cans. There is so much commotion going on that none of us see the car coming up the street, as Lila steps off the curb and tries to stop apples and oranges from rolling away.

The car screeches. Lila trips and falls on her back. Mom screams. Michael runs to Lila. The driver of the car is now kneeling over Lila, crying how sorry he is. Moms checks to see if Lila is OK. People are walking by and stopping. A crowd starts to build up. As horrible as it sounds, if she's hurt or not, I know she's going to milk this for all its worth. I turn my back on all of them, walk away, and go home. Whatever the case, it will be my fault.

It's over an hour since I left everyone downstairs. Mom just walked in. She heads for the kitchen first, and drops the two shopping bags on the counter with a large thud. I've already made up my mind; I'm not going to say I'm sorry to her. Mom stands in the doorway. She's boiling mad!

"You have a very serious problem. Your temper is out of control. Lila could have been seriously hurt. Thank God, it's only a little bruise. And, poor Michael, how could you treat him that way? Shame on you, Sarah. I am telling you now that this craziness with Lila has to stop, once and for all. If not, I swear I am going to take you to see a doctor."

"Mom, didn't you see what I saw? Lila was all over Michael. She's going to try to take him away from me. I know her. And I won't let her. He's my friend, not hers, he's mine! But you know what the worst part is? Lila goes out of her way, over and over, to make me miserable, to hurt me, and you never see that, never! And that hurts me even more." My voice cracks and the tears come streaming down my face. Mom stares at me, looking helpless.

"Sarah, I am sorry for your pain. Perhaps I will never

understand or know what goes on between the two of you, but I cannot abandon her. I worry about what goes on in that apartment. Daddy says I worry too much, making a mountain out of a molehill. But I can't help feeling that something is not right. Someone has to keep an eye out for her."

"But why does it have to be you? Why don't you keep an eye out for me?"

"That's not fair. Listen—I will try to be more understanding towards you but you have to, for your own sake, stop being so angry. It is not healthy and there is nothing to gain from hate. And I think you should apologize to Michael."

Mom leaves. I listen and wait till I can leave the apartment without her hearing me. As soon as it's clear, I make my getaway and go out into the hallway. I march down to Lila's apartment, ring the doorbell. She opens the door. There is a Band-Aid on her left cheek. I flick my finger on her shoulder, hard enough to surprise her, and she jerks backwards.

"Stay clear of Michael. You'll end up hurting him. I won't let that happen!"

As I walk away, Lila steps out in the hallway. "By the way, thanks for asking how I am," she says sarcastically.

I stop in my tracks, raise my middle finger to her. "You're still alive aren't you?"

Back in my room, I close the door and take out a piece of construction paper from my desk. With a black crayon, I write in large letters a note for Michael. When I'm finished, I tape it to the window. I AM SO SORRY. PLEASE FORGIVE ME!

Michael

After The Chaos

I can't stop shaking. Between Lila's surprise seduction, Sarah's blowup, Lila’s almost getting hit by a car, food scattered all over the street—it was so crazy! If you were standing across the street or looking out a window, we must have looked like the Keystone Cops from the silent movies. I'm tired and confused. All I want to do is just close my eyes and pretend that none of today happened, but it did and now I'm feeling lousy, guilty and dumb!

All the way home from Maestro's, I kept thinking to myself that Lila wasn't so bad, not at all like Sarah said. I liked walking home with her. She was nice and funny. By the time we got to our block, I almost didn't want to say goodbye.

But then everything changed when we got to Sarah and Lila's building. There was no way I could have been prepared for Lila pressing her body to mine. The way she held on to me was very grown up. And when she blew in my ear and said those words, I realized that Lila wasn't just flirting. It was something more, but I didn't know what. It's not like I've had any experience with girls besides Sarah, and we're just friends. Lila definitely was acting like she wanted something else. But what? Maybe she was testing me. Did she guess there was something different about me?

That's when I broke out in a cold sweat, and then Sarah came around the corner and all hell broke loose!

Seeing Lila and me together, the way we were, made Sarah livid. Her face got all twisted and the tone of her voice sent chills down my spine. Right then and there, I felt like I was the most horrible person in the world. I wanted to explain, but everything was happening too fast. From the time Sarah and Hannah came around the block and the car almost hit Lila, I don't think more than a few seconds passed.

Meanwhile, a group of about twenty people had gathered around to see what was going on. Almost immediately, they were all yelling out their opinions.

"Don't move her! Put her head up."

"No, keep her head down."

"Can she move her legs, arms?"

"Don't touch her, wait till the ambulance comes."

"Don't let the driver go. The police will have to question him."

"Someone called the police?"

Finally the driver, an elderly man, was sitting on the sidewalk with his head in his hands, praying. He got up and shouted out for God to forgive him! All the attention went from Lila to the man. He was breathing so hard. For sure I thought he was going to have a heart attack. Then, to everyone's surprise, Lila, with the help of Hannah, slowly got up and went over to the man, took his hands in hers, and held them up to her cheek.

"I am not hurt. Please do not worry. Go home. It was my fault. I should not have run out into the street the way I did. Please forgive me."

Lila kisses his hands and helps him to his car. The man, sobbing with relief and gratitude, drove off. Everyone then clapped their hands. I think I even heard someone cry.

"What an angel she is! A gift is what she is," says someone.

Lila lets Hannah take her by the arm, and they walk up the stairs. Before they enter the building, Lila turns around and waves her hand like a wand. People again clapped their hands, this time softly, and wished her luck. The door closed behind them. For some reason, I got the sense that Sarah might have been watching the whole bizarre scene from Tar Beach. I looked up but thankfully she wasn't there.

Once in my room, I plop down on my bed. My mind is spinning. What I can't stop thinking about is, did Lila plan for Sarah to see us? If she did, how could she know when they would be coming home? Was she just hoping she'd get lucky? That would have been downright mean and calculating. But she was so kind to the man, so sensitive and generous. I don't know what to think. I could tell that everyone who was out there today thought that Lila Rosen was, indeed, an angel.

Having friends is complicated, hard. Maybe I should go back to being a loner. A cold breeze comes in from my window. I get up to close it. What's that on Sarah's window? I put my head out to get a closer look. There's a sign with big black letters. I read it. She forgives me.

The next morning, Sarah is waiting for me in front of my building. We walk to school together and talk about yesterday. I tell her I'm sorry that I hurt her feelings.

"It wasn't your fault. You're just too sweet and totally inexperienced about girls like Lila. Trust me, Michael, there is so much stuff you need to learn and I'm the person to teach it to you."

Sarah walks me to my class. After we hug and arrange to meet after school, I feel so relieved, happy. I'm hoping Sarah does, too.

December

Sarah

New Year's Eve Morning

I wake up to the sound of Mom singing along with Conway Twitty's “It's Only Make Believe” and the clanking of metal pans. The smell of coffee and a roast beef in the oven make it impossible to stay in bed any longer. My clock says it's only six-thirty in the morning. Mom must have gotten up at the crack of dawn. I better get my behind moving to see if I can help her with anything before I go to school. Lots to do today, because tonight is New Year's Eve and Michael's fourteenth birthday. And, to top it all off, surprise of all surprises, Mr. and Mrs. Stein are coming to our party!

When I told Mom that it was Michael's birthday on New Year's Eve, she insisted that we invite him and his parents. I stared at her like she had lost her mind. "Are you crazy? His parents don't go anywhere, ever!"

"Well, something has changed with the Stein family, because Judith Stein, is out and about all the time now. A few days after the Tar Beach episode, we were in the same line at the butcher's. From the second she introduced herself to me, I knew we were going to be friends. I liked her right away. And of course, she is very grateful to you."

"For what?" I ask, filled with pride.

"For being Michael's friend. She said she has never seen him happier."

I kind of knew all this because Michael told me all about the night that his mother stood up to his father. He didn't go into details, but he said his mother announced that things were going to be different. I wanted Michael to understand what had happened, so I told him, "You know, Michael, my mom says that every once in a while a woman has to put a man in his place, let him know who's the boss. And that's exactly what your mother did."

"Sarah, my mother isn't like yours and my father isn't like other men."

"I get that but, still, you're not so serious now and your mother is becoming friends with everyone. And isn't your father just a teeny bit different now?"

"Maybe but just a little. At supper, he actually talks and sometimes he even tells a joke. The thing is that I'm never sure when the other shoe is going to drop, know what I mean?"

I said “yes” but I really didn't. Mr. and Mrs. Stein weren't like any other parents I knew. The Steins were mysterious. "Michael, you have to be positive. I bet your father has turned a new leaf and you can't see it yet." I said this with all the confidence I could muster. I'm not sure I believed what I said, and the way that Michael looked at me told me that it would be better if I dropped the subject.

A few nights ago, Mom, Dad, and I were sitting, watching "The Comedy Hour" with Lucy and Desi. My dad loves Lucy. Usually, he cracks up from the minute she comes on till the end of the show. But that night he wasn't laughing. He didn't even seem to be listening. During one of the commercials, I nudged Mom and pointed to Dad.

"Leo, you OK? You're not sick, are you?"

"Hannah, I'm fine but I got a bad feeling about the Steins coming over for New Year's Eve. I don't know if it's such a good idea," said Dad, sounding really anxious.

"Don't make a big deal about this. Everything will be OK."

"Hannah, our friends are nice people and I got a hunch that Stein might not be so comfortable with people like Dudley. Then there's also Fritzy. You never know what's gonna come out of her mouth! Nah, I got a bad feeling about this."

"Leo, Dudley can take care of himself, and, as far as Fritzy, well, let's cross our fingers she keeps her mouth shut."

"From God's mouth to your ear. It's just that I don't want him insulting Dudley. That man is too good a friend to us. If Stein says anything out of line, I'll have to do something about it. Want you to know that up front."

We continued on, watching the show, but doubt had set in and none of us laughed at Lucy and Desi. Dad's words were a downer, and I started to imagine all the things that could go wrong. Not everyone is OK with being around a Negro. I was a good example of that when I first met Dudley. And, Fritzy, she's so mean and ugly, she could easily make Mr. Stein want to leave the party. Then there's Lila. We had managed to get through Thanksgiving without any drama. We were both on our best behavior for Mom. But with Lila, you never know what she has up her sleeve.

Michael and I haven't talked about Lila since we made up. I caused him to feel bad enough. Besides I can't keep harping about her. That gets boring. And I never want to be accused of being boring, God forbid! But tonight, we're all going to be with one another for a long time. I can try to keep him away from her, but that's not going to be so easy. But I'm sure as hell going to try.

Before I get dressed, I open my window and look up at the sky. If I ever needed God's help, it's going to be tonight. I place my hands in my lap and close my eyes.

I pray, "Dear God, I know I only talk to you when I'm really worried. And I would understand if you didn't want to pay any attention to me. But, if you can, just keep an eye out for Michael and Dudley tonight. It would mean a whole lot to me and to Mom and Dad. I just want Michael to have a birthday that he will always remember, and not one he will want to forget. Thank you from someone who deep inside believes that you care and listen to everyone, including me, even if I'm not so deserving."

Michael

New Year's Eve Morning

Father is sitting at the kitchen table, watching Mother with what I guess is surprise or wonder. I'm not sure which. When I look at her, I can see why. Mother is busy moving so quickly it's hard to keep up with her. She's going back and forth from the stove to the oven to the fridge, all the while rattling on and on about how much she likes Hannah Lanin and Sarah. It's as if she's roller skating from one end of the kitchen to the other. Mother sees me, stops, and showers me with kisses

"Happy Birthday, my beautiful son! Fourteen years old. You are practically a grown man!"

I'm not fourteen yet, my birthday is officially at 12 midnight, New Year's Eve. My birthdays have always been quiet. There would be a cake and a sensible present, breakfast in bed, but then it was over. But this birthday will be different because Sarah is determined to make it special.

Mother continues to speak to Father as she goes about preparing breakfast. "I am so excited, Joseph. Why we haven't been to a party since Germany, before the war. Remember how much fun we used to have?"

"Judith, you know how I feel about such things."

"Joseph, it can't always be your way. I think it was lovely

for the Lanins to invite us to celebrate New Year's Eve and especially to celebrate Michael's birthday too, very gracious."

Father takes his eyes off Mother and slowly turns his attention to me.

"This is your doing, isn't it?" he says, accusingly.

I can hear the slow grinding of father's teeth. My eyes quickly search for his hands. I can't see them. Are they clenched? Is he reaching for his belt? Do I just stand here and take it or do I stand up to him like Mother did? If he's going to do anything, it's going to be real soon. My mind is racing faster than I can think. I stand up straight, prepared for his next move, when out of the blue Mother starts to sing *Auld Lang Syne* in German. The unexpected sweetness of her voice forces both Father and me to stop and stare at her in amazement. She places a platter of toast and scrambled eggs on the table, then a pot of coffee. Still singing, she takes a pair of potholders, opens the oven door, and takes out a beautiful streusel coffee cake, which she proudly holds up in the air and then places in the center of the kitchen table.

"Now, Joseph, don't even think of getting up from the table. When you finish your eggs, you will have a piece of this streusel, and we will drink our coffee. Then the three of us will talk about tonight. Michael, sit down, please."

I feel like I'm watching a movie. I stare at my parents—Mother is as happy as a lark and Father looks like the wind has been taken out of him. All of this seems too good to be true. Part of me is still suspicious.

It's true that in the last two months Mother has become another person. No longer does she sleep the day away. Now she gets up in the morning, makes my breakfast, and packs a lunch for school. While I eat, she tells me her plans for the day. At least once a week she and Mrs. Lanin have coffee together and talk about whatever mothers talk about. She goes out for long walks and shops for food, always coming home with something special for Father.

On Saturdays, Mother is again picking me up from my violin lessons, taking extra time to spend with the Maestro and the Signora. It is as if she had never stopped. They are happy to see her, and no mention is made as to why she stopped coming. Afterwards we go to a movie or take the train to the Grand Concourse, where all the big stores are. Mother has taken to window shopping and buys me whatever I want or what she thinks I would like. Now I go to school wearing clothes like all the other boys.

Father has been acting different, too. Now, he talks at supper and asks both of us about our day. We answer and he politely listens. He never brings up work anymore because that would mean complaints and Mother doesn't want to hear that. One night he started to tell us about a man he thinks doesn't belong on the job, and Mother stopped him right away.

"Joseph, I refuse to hear anything negative. I only want to hear about good things. It is important that we take this time to enjoy each other, something we have not been able to do in a long time."

I believe Father's been trying, but, right now, I'm pretty sure he's reached his limit. Mother sips her coffee and takes a bite of the streusel. Up to this point, I think she's been ignoring Father's discontent, but Mother acts like everything is fine.

"Look, Joseph, I know that you're not thrilled about going to this party. I am fully aware that socializing is not easy for you anymore, but Michael and I would be happy if you join us. If it will be too difficult for you, I understand. Michael and I can just go on our own."

Mother has finished all of her eggs, streusel, and coffee but Father and I have hardly touched our plates. Without a word, Father gets up from his chair and leaves the kitchen. Mother looks at me and throws her hands up in the air. "What can I do? I tried. Oh well, we'll just have to have a good time without him!" To my surprise, Mother says this with a blasé attitude, as if it made no difference to her at all.

Sarah

New Year's Eve

"Sarah, am I talking to the wall or what? People will be here any minute. Get moving!" Mom yells from the kitchen.

I check myself in the mirror one last time. After changing into four different outfits, I've finally decided on a pair of black cigarette pants, a new white lace blouse, and ballet slippers. With my hair piled up on my head, I look very French, just like Bridget Bardot, the movie star - at least that's what Darlene tells me. Mom for sure isn't going to be crazy about this new look, and I know she's not going to like the blue eye shadow and eyeliner I put on. Maybe, with all the excitement going on, with the Steins coming, she won't even notice.

God, I hope Michael thinks I look great. When we first met, all I wanted was to be best friends, but after the last few months, I feel so much more, and hope he does, too. For his birthday I am going to give him a kiss, a real one, like the ones Lila and I used to practice.

As soon as I walk into the living room, Dad sees me and gives me a long whistle. "Boy, oh boy, Hannah, come look at your little girl! What a beauty!"

Mom is standing at the table, arranging platters of mini

roast beef sandwiches. As soon as she sees me, her hands take the position at her hips, never a good sign.

"Hmm!" she says, as she examines my face. "I didn't know we invited Cleopatra tonight. No, my darling, you go march into the bathroom and wash that all off, now!" As I turn to go, the doorbell rings.

Everyone walks in at one time, holding a platter of something stuffed. If there is a hole that can be made into a piece of bread, a fruit, or a vegetable, it gets stuffed. Tomatoes, little potatoes, olives, celery, eggs, filled with different kinds of mystery dip. Then there are the roll-ups: salami, salmon, cheese, all filled with sour cream, cream cheese, and God knows what else. My favorites are the canapés that come with gherkins standing straight up like miniature soldiers.

In the living room, four bridge tables are set up for food and one for desserts, which can be anything from cakes, cookies, cupcakes, chocolates, and Fritzy's famous Jell-O mold. Every year Fritzy makes one in a different color. So far, it's been yellow, orange, blue, purple, and green. And each year, she folds in fruits, nuts, a vegetable or sometimes all three. Last year, someone placed a bet with Dad that there were sardines in it. As far as I can remember, no one has ever eaten it. Two years ago, Mom felt bad for Fritzy and embarrassed for Lila so she came up with the brilliant idea of letting Fritzy believe that it was always such a masterpiece that it was too beautiful to eat.

"Your Jell-O mold will always have its place of honor as the centerpiece for the desert table," Mother would say graciously. This has kept Fritzy quiet at New Year's and proud as a peacock. Meanwhile, everyone is laughing behind her back. Max just ignores the whole thing but I know it embarrasses Lila.

In minutes, the living room is filled. The only ones who haven't arrived yet are Michael and his parents and the Rosens. Where is he? God, I hope nothing's wrong.

Suddenly the room is filled with oohs and ahs! Fritzy walks in with Max behind her, holding this year's surprise Jell-O mold. Fritzy takes it from Max, and places it in the center of the dessert table. She stands back, admiring her creation as does everyone else. This year the mold is pink and white. Inside are large red strawberries. On top is 1960 spelled out in red and pink jelly beans. To everyone's surprise, it's not only beautiful but it looks good enough to eat!

"Well, well, Mrs. Rosen, if this isn't the prettiest thing I have ever seen," Dudley says, giving her his best gracious smile, his two gold teeth sparkling.

Fritzy mumbles a thank you, and everybody claps their hands. The party is off to a good start. Dad gets busy mixing drinks, Dudley puts on some records and people start to dance. Everyone is here except Lila and the Steins. Maybe something happened. I'm getting nervous; I feel a zit coming out on the middle of my forehead. Shit! I'm about to go into the bathroom to put some Clearasil on it when the door opens and Mrs. Stein walks in. Mom goes over to her right away, takes her hand and starts introducing her to everyone. I keep looking at the door—there's no Michael or Mr. Stein. My zit is growing by the second. I gotta go. As soon as I turn around, I crash right into Minnie who is holding a plate stacked with mini sweet and sour meatballs and something else that is orange. Her plate lands on my beautiful new white lace blouse.

"*Oi, gevald,* Sarah. Where's the fire?" Minnie asks hysterically. I feel everyone's eyes on me and then I hear Lila laughing.

"Oh, Sarah, I can't believe what a spaz you are!"

I spin around and there she is, looking tall, slim, graceful, and more beautiful than I will ever be. Lila walks up to me and, with her pinkie, daintily scoops up a small meatball which had landed right in the middle of my chest, between my breasts. She gobbles it up and turns around. Talk about being humiliated! Who should be standing right behind her, but Michael, his eyes popping out and his mouth open!

"Michael, you have to have one, these are crazy delicious!"

I push Lila out of my way, causing her to stumble backwards, right into Michael's arms.

I just can't win. I run past everyone, out the door, and up to Tar Beach. Mom's worried voice echoing after me. Any minute

Lila will be apologizing to Mom for making me upset, that she didn't mean it, but she did. She loved every minute of it.

It doesn't take long for Michael to come up after me. I sit back against the concrete roof ledge and curl myself into a ball, hoping that he won't see me in the dark and will go away. But no such luck.

"Sarah, you OK?"

My first impulse is to ignore him but I'm dying to know how it happened that they showed up together. Was it planned? Why the hell didn't he come to my rescue when she pulled the stunt with the meatball?

"I don't know, Michael, what do you think?"

The words come shooting out of my mouth in such a nasty way that even I'm surprised at how ugly I sound. Michael ignores my horrible attitude and bends down to lovingly cover my shoulders with a coat. He slides down next to me and moves as close as he can till we are shoulder to shoulder, hip to hip, knee to knee, foot to foot, toe to toe, making our bodies feel like one.

Once again I'm reminded of how much I love him. I make up my mind that it's now or never. I want him to know. I get up first and pull him up to me. Letting the coat fall to the floor, I stand on my toes and draw him close to my body. With eyes closed, I think back to how Lila taught me to kiss a boy and to make sure he never forgot it

"Sarah, pretend the boy you're kissing is a sugar cone filled with your favorite ice cream. It's so delicious that you want it to last forever. So you take your time licking it a little bit here and there, your tongue circling the cone. When you think you can't stand it any longer you softly and sweetly rest your lips on his and . . . linger."

By the time I have my tongue in his mouth, Michael's body starts to tremble; the softness of his body tightens up and becomes awkwardly firm. His hands slowly remove mine from his neck and places them down at my side. We both shrink back a little, not knowing what to do next.

All at once the memory of shame and guilt that I experienced with Lila comes over me. I walk away and sit on the ledge looking up at the sky. I want to cry, but I've made him feel bad again. I should just tell him I'm sorry for being so forward, sorry for being such a bitch this evening and will he please forgive me, again! But Michael, who proves to be, as always, so much better than me, comes towards me with my coat and a kind smile.

"Hey, I think we should go down now. I'm starving and we can't let Lila finish all those meatballs."

His words fill me with relief. Everything is going to be fine. Then I challenge him to race me downstairs.

Michael

Sarah's Kiss

With Sarah's arms around my neck and her soft lips on mine, the sounds of New Year's Eve, the crowds of people laughing, singing, dancing, the tooting of noisemakers, and my heart racing, everything becomes muffled. The sweetness and warmth of her kisses fill me with an unexpected emotion, but suddenly something changes. Her lips press a bit harder, her arms tighten on my neck. I have no idea what is happening. I try to let go, but then Sarah thrusts her tongue deep into my mouth, and my whole body goes into shock. Sarah feels my discomfort, too. I remove her hands from my neck and put them at her side. She looks as confused as I am. The last thing I want to do is make her feel bad. Sarah is the best person in my life and I can't lose her.

The noise from the street soars up to Tar Beach, snapping us out of the puzzling moment and making us also aware of how really cold it is and that we're both shivering. We both look into each other's eyes and without saying a word, we realize that the strangeness of what just happened is over for now. Maybe tomorrow or next week we'll talk about it or we'll just let it pass. But for now, it's New Year's Eve and my birthday, and I'm spending it with my best friend.

Sarah

Back At The Party

Michael and I come back to the party as if nothing had happened. The party is in full swing and everyone is having a good time. I turn to look for Lila and she's staring right at me. I pay no attention to her. Mom comes to me and asks if I'm OK.

"Never better," I say, meaning every word.

"Well, that's good to know, now go change your blouse and get something to eat. You have to be starving."

Feeling just a tiny bit rebellious, I decide I don't want to and say so. She doesn't look happy and gives me one of her not now looks.

"Ok, have it your way but no more *tsuris* tonight!"

When Mom’s turned away, Michael says with a laugh, "Sarah, go change, orange is just not your color."

I look down at my shirt and know he's right. I leave and come back in a few minutes in a white sweater. Michael comes towards me to take my hand just as Lila glides up to him and asks him to dance. He very politely says, “No." Oh boy, Lila is about to have a fit. I am loving this. Lila is not used to hearing the word no, especially from boys. Before I can relish Lila's moment of rejection, Michael takes me to the middle of the living room and we begin to dance.

We're so in step with each other that it seems like we've been dancing together forever. Now, not only is Lila staring at us but everyone else is, too. Michael is the center of attention, as is Mrs. Stein. All the men are eyeing her, Daddy included. She is so pretty. It's a given that, even if he looks like his father, if Michael takes after anyone, it's his mother. Which reminds me that Michael and his Mother have come without Mr. Stein. I'll have to ask him about that tomorrow, but not now. I don't want to spoil anything, we're having too much of a good time.

Crazy. It's hard to believe that just a little while ago I thought it was the end of the world and now everything is perfect. I catch Mom staring at me, pointing to the food, signaling me to eat.

At the food table, I pick up a mini roast beef sandwich and pop it into my mouth. As soon as it goes down, I reach for another one and am about to eat it when Lila comes up behind me.

"Keep eating like that and you'll never lose your baby fat," she says, cheerfully.

I turn to face her and, without any hesitation, I inhale the sandwich like I'm a vacuum cleaner. Then I go for the cherry tomato stuffed with white "gunk" and eat that in one bite. I rub my tummy and give her a huge grin.

"Lila, I have to tell you something. You can't insult me anymore tonight. As a matter of fact, from this minute on, I do not see you, I do not hear you. As far as I'm concerned you do not exist!"

I grab another two mini sandwiches, walk over to Michael, and feed them to him as if he's a baby. We both start to giggle. Lila is beside herself with anger. Furious, she marches over to her father and says something to him but he pays no attention. He, like every other man at the party has his eyes fixed on Mrs. Stein and Dudley dancing together. Lila tugs at her father's sleeve and angrily says something to him. I bet she's asking to leave. Lila's second rejection of the evening comes as Max whispers something in her ear that only makes her more infuriated. As Lila leaves the apartment, a round of applause breaks out. Mrs. Stein and Dudley take a bow.

Sam, Howie Rothman's dad, yells out. "Now that's what I call dancing! That's a hell of a cha-cha the two of you did. As good as Ginger Rogers and Fred Astaire." I guess everyone agrees because the applause gets louder.

Sam, without a doubt, has had too many Seven and Sevens. He walks over to the stack of records, looks through them, and holds one up in the air. "Ok people; let's have a little dance contest. And as a special prize, the winners get to take home Fritzy's Jell-O mold!" Now everyone goes nuts laughing. Sam turns to Dad and hands him the record.

"Leo, would you do the honor, please?"

When the needle touches the vinyl, something wonderful happens. Michael and I, as if we are reading each other's mind, move towards Dudley and Mrs. Stein. Michael takes his mother's hand and I take Dudley's. The four of us dance and the room goes crazy wild. Nearing the end of the record, we switch partners and I'm back with Michael and Mrs. Stein with Dudley.

I'm happier this second than I have ever been in my life. As Michael spins me around, I spot Max walking out the door, clearly offended. Fritzy, fit to be tied, is behind him, carrying her Jell-O mold.

No one has made a big deal of the Rosens leaving, except maybe Mom, who always feels bad for Max and Lila. I know she wants to say something to me, but there's no time because something draws her attention towards the doorway. Standing there is Mr. Stein staring at his wife dancing with Dudley. The expression of disgust and disbelief on his face sends chills up my spine. The four of us stop dancing. Dad stops the record. Except for Guy Lombardo and his band playing on TV, everything and everyone have stopped moving and the room goes deathly still.

Michael quickly moves to his mother's side. Mom takes a breath and walks up to Mr. Stein and greets him with her most beautiful and welcoming smile, takes him by the elbow, and guides him into the living room. Mr. Stein flinches at Mom's touch but that doesn't stop her from chatting away and introducing him to everybody as if it's the most natural thing for him to be here. I decide to do as Mom does and come up to him and introduce myself. But Michael's father ignores me. He's overwhelmed with everything he is seeing. He's now standing in the center of the room, his eyes wandering over the tables of leftover food, empty and full glasses of alcohol, party hats, and faces of people who are all strangers to him.

Dad and Dudley walk up to Mr. Stein and introduce themselves. They both put out their hands for a handshake, but Mr. Stein, repulsed at the sight of Dudley's black hand, steps away from them. Dad looks miffed but Mr. Stein's rudeness doesn't seem to bother Dudley at all, because he starts praising what great dancers his son and wife are and what an honor it is to have danced with Mrs. Stein. Now I'm scared. Mr. Stein looks as if he would like nothing better than to smash his fist into Dudley's face. He quickly puts his hands in his pants pockets, trying to control them from acting on their own. Mrs. Stein quickly steps between them. She whispers something in Mr. Stein's ear. Suddenly Mr. Stein goes from someone who is about to violently blow up to a small brooding boy. Now it's everyone else's turn to be shocked. Mrs. Stein thanks Mom for a wonderful party but they have to leave.

"But we still have Michael's birthday cake," Mom says.

Mrs. Stein lowers her eyes and is able to send some kind of message to Mom. It's understood that he will stay and celebrate his birthday. And, just like that, his father and mother are gone.

"Well, I'll be a son of a bitch," says Dad, "Hannah, I told you."

"Not now, Leo." Mom answers in a stern voice.

Minutes later, everything is back to normal, and it's five minutes away from midnight. Dad shuts the lights off in the living room, while Mom and I bring out Michael's birthday cake with fourteen lit candles. I stand next to Michael and we interlock our fingers. Guy Lombardo is calling the countdown as the glittering ball comes down on TV.

"Five, four, three, two, one, Happy New Year!"

Michael blows out the candles. Shouts of hooray, happy birthday, happy New Year fill the room. All at once the lights come back on and Michael loosens his fingers from mine. Right away he's swamped by wet kisses and embraces from the women, and manly slaps on the back from the men.

I watch Michael as he accepts the sincere blessings from the people around him. I watch as his face struggles to smile. Mom and I catch each other's eye, and we both watch Michael as he leaves.

Michael

Another Revelation

Once out of the apartment I run downstairs and outside to my building. Even though I'm just next door, I'm having a hard time squeezing my way through groups of people on the sidewalk still celebrating the New Year. I elbow my way out, saying, excuse me, and finally get into my building and sprint up the stairs as fast as I can. All I can think is that I have to stop father before he does any harm to mother and makes her give in to him. If that happens, we go back to the way it was and I can't let that happen.

To my surprise, the door is unlocked. I'm half expecting Father to be waiting for me in the dark but the room is empty. I walk to my parents' door and stand as close as I dare. I tilt my head and press my ear to the door and listen for voices, or cries, but I hear nothing.

Is it possible they're not here? Where are they? Something is not right.

I can't decide if I should call out Mother's name or just storm into their bedroom, but something is stopping me, fear of what I'll find . . . I don't know. I'll just wait a few seconds. I sit down outside the door and put my head between my knees, trying to stop the urge to scream out. Wait, I hear something. It's Mother. She's speaking so low I can't make out what she's saying. She must be hurt. I jump up, and turn the door knob. I hear a cry so tormented that my hand jerks free from the doorknob as if it's a hot torch. My body starts to shake as I realize that the voice full of pain does not belong to Mother but to Father.

Part Two

1960

January – April

January

Lila

On New Year's Day Morning

Never went to sleep. Too busy thinking, plotting. Have a major headache. Need some aspirin—but to get that I have to leave my room. I'm not ready to come out yet and greet the new year or Mom and especially Daddy. I'm more than just a little angry at him. I heard him last night try to jiggle the doorknob to my room, but I locked it, serves him right. When I told him I wanted to leave the party, he didn't even ask me why. He was too busy along with all the other men, acting like they were bewitched by Mrs. Stein. In the beginning of the evening, I was jealous only of Sarah and Michael. But then there was Mrs. Stein. That was unexpected. Anyhow it was a terrible night and I wasn't too upset to see the year end. I hope 1960 is going to be better than 1959.

"Lila, *mach shnel*, before I *plotz*," Mom shouts from the kitchen.

There is nothing ever soft or quiet about her. Her footsteps are heavy, and her voice is rough and always sounds crabby. Daddy must be gone because she never raises her voice when he's around. I drag myself out of bed and into the kitchen. Mom is standing by the sink, tapping her fingers, her cheeks flushed with excitement. She orders me to sit down.

"So, what's so important?" I ask her.

"Everybody is talking about what happened last night at Hannah's after we left. By this time the whole neighborhood probably knows. Some party it was, oh boy!"

Mom exaggerates everything she sees and hears. I guess I don't look too interested in what she has to tell me because she takes three giant steps towards me and yanks at my ponytail hard.

"Ok, Ok! What's the latest gossip?" I ask.

Mom sits down across from me, spreads her beefy hands on the table, and gives me a smile that is wide enough to expose her two gold teeth and a whole bunch of silver fillings in the back of her mouth. Ughhh, so nauseating in the morning!

"So, after we left last night, Mr. Stein shows up and sees his wife dancing with Hannah's *schvartza*. He was so *meshuge* that he pulled him away from his wife and beat him up. Punching, kicking, the whole thing. What a fight everyone said. Next, he drags that shameful wife of his out of the apartment! She was screaming so loud that people in the street thought he was going to kill her!"

"Who told you that?"

"Lila, do I need to clean out your ears or something. I just told you—everyone! For all we know, Stein's wife could be dead right now!"

I stare at her. Her eyes are on fire, and she looks like she's won money on the weekly numbers. As much as I hate her, I can't believe that she would be so thrilled about someone getting killed. I shake my head in disgust. “Please tell me I'm imagining this whole conversation.”

"*Gottenyu*, and that poor boy Michael, what if Stein hurt him too? Maybe I should call police . . . what you think?" Mom springs up from her chair as if she's fifty pounds lighter and reaches for the telephone. I jump up and pull her hand away.

"STOP IT! You're acting insane! If anyone is dead, the police would be all over the street and in the Steins’ building and ours, questioning everyone who was at the party last night. Mom, you have to stop spreading rumors. One day you'll get into real trouble."

Mom turns to me. She's so angry at me that her face

becomes distorted. "You don't say! Well, if anything bad happened last night, it will be all Hannah's fault."

I can't listen anymore; she's out of her mind. "All right, you think whatever you want," I say in frustration. "I'm going back to bed."

But I'm not getting off that easy. Mom puts her face close to mine. I can smell the coffee and the licorice candy on her breath. "Yeah, go stick up for your Hannah. You and your father, always taking her side."

She's waiting for me to say something, but I'm not going to give her the satisfaction. Still in my pajamas, I move away from her and walk out of the apartment and cross the hall. I ring the Lanins' doorbell. Sarah opens the door.

"What do you want?" She looks at me as if I'm poison.

"My mother thinks that Mr. Stein may have killed Mrs. Stein and hurt Michael. She wants to call the police. I thought I should tell your mom."

"Lila, you and your mother are both nuts!" Sarah slams the door in my face.

I hear Hannah's voice in the background. I wait. Hannah opens the door. "Lila, sweetheart, you can tell your mother that no one is dead. Mrs. Stein is alive and well and so is Michael."

"I know that. It's just that she says that the whole neighborhood is talking about what happened last night. Is it true that Mr. Stein beat up your friend Dudley?"

"No, it is not true. Nothing like that happened. Mr. Stein came and took his wife home. Michael went soon after. Mr. Dudley left after him. That's it!"

"Ok, I guess I'll go home now."

Hannah looks like she wants me to come inside but she hesitates. She turns—Sarah is standing in the middle of the living room. Her eyes are saying, "Don't you dare." Hannah takes me in her arms and whispers Happy New Year. The door closes. I look towards my apartment but I don't want to go back in there. I can hear Mom talking on the phone, spreading her lies, adding to the rumor mill. Most people don't listen to her but that never stops her.

I'm starting to break out again; the ugly bumps are

flowering. They hurt. I run up the steps to the roof and push open the door to Tar Beach. An icy wind welcomes me. If I stay here long enough, maybe I'll get lucky and my body will go numb. That way I won't be able to feel anything anymore.

Michael

One Week Later

There is no doubt in my mind that, after Father left with Mother on New Year's Eve, everyone at the Lanins' was frightened by him. But not me. Never again. Today I am going to tell Mother I am giving up the violin, that I want to be an artist. Then I will tell Father. That night, when I came home and heard him crying in the darkness, I discovered something about him that I never thought possible - he's human and has fears like everyone else.

To my surprise, on the first morning of the New Year, Father let me know in so many words that Mother needed to rest for a few days, and he was going to take care of supper and whatever I needed. He spoke to me in a voice I hadn't heard before. It was kind.

Father is usually gone by the time I get up for school, but he leaves me a simple breakfast of cereal, a piece of fruit, and money for lunch. When he comes home from work, he brings Chinese or deli for dinner. He makes a plate for Mother and takes it into her.

At supper, it's just Father and me. He asks me questions - about my day, my music, and then, when he can't think of anything else to say, he reads his newspaper and I read a book. When we finish eating, he insists on cleaning the dishes and tells me to go study. I like it this way. It's almost like we're two old men who have been enemies forever and now have come to a truce. After he's done, he leaves the kitchen, turns off the lights, and goes into the bedroom to be with Mother.

Mother has been in her bedroom for a whole week. I've had a lot of time to think the last few days, and I've decided that, if I wait for her to come out into the world again, I might lose my nerve. So this morning I knock softly on Mother's door and, before she can answer, I walk in with tea and toast on a tray. To my surprise she's sitting up in bed, her hair brushed, and her face shiny from being washed, and she is smiling. I feel like she's been waiting for me.

"Good morning, Mother, I've brought you some breakfast. Can we talk? I have something to tell you."

"Oh, Michael, I want to talk to you too. Can I go first please?"

Mother says this with so much excitement that it almost scares me. I put the tray down on her night table and stand there staring at her.

"Michael, come, come sit by me, there is so much I need to tell you."

I sit down by her side. She reaches for my hands and holds them in hers. Her eyes look deeply into mine. "I know you think I have deserted you again, selfishly escaping into myself, sleeping the time away, but I haven't. Instead, I have been trying to figure out how to tell you some truths about myself and about your father.

Wait a minute, why does this feel like we have changed roles? It's as if I'm the parent and Mother is the child. I can't imagine what she is going to reveal.

"First, I want to apologize. The last few years I have behaved selfishly. I have let my dark moods take over. I am also aware that I have not been the best of mothers. Sadly, I am not even sure when I gave up."

"Mother, It's not your fault that you get sick sometimes. You can't help it."

"No, please, you of all people do not need to make excuses

for me. As a Mother, I have been irresponsible and selfish. I hope that, in time, you might be able to forgive me - us."

Right now, I'm not sure that I want to hear anything. Maybe it's better if I know nothing. Besides, I wanted this talk to be about me.

"Michael, are you OK?"

"Sure," I say with resentment.

Mother is surprised by the tone of my voice. I've made her feel bad. "I am sorry, Mother. Please go ahead."

Mother takes a moment. "Thank you. Michael. Remember when your father stood in the doorway of the Lanins' apartment on New Year's Eve?"

"Yes."

"What did you see?"

"He looked afraid." I say it without any hesitation.

"Well, you are right. When he saw us dancing and laughing with the very same people he has tried to keep us away from, he became frightened. In his mind, he realized that he could actually lose me. When we left the Lanins', he held on to me so tightly that I thought he might hurt me - or you. I prayed that you would stay at the party so that he would not harm you, too. But as soon as we got home, your father broke down and cried liked a baby, begging me not to leave him. Then for the first time, your father spoke about things that he has never had the courage to reveal and I had never wanted to hear."

"Like what?" I ask with curiosity.

"Michael, your father has been living with a lie for years, one that has been eating away at him."

Mother slowly gets out of bed and walks to the window. She pulls up the shade and lets the winter sun come dancing into the room. She spreads her arms out to embrace the sun and does a pirouette. The lightness of the moment lasts only seconds before she pulls the shade back down.

"So much easier to tell hard truths when it is not so bright, don't you think?"

"I guess," I answer, not knowing what else to say.

She leans over and softly strokes my head. I wait for her to begin.

"Your father has kept a secret from me, one that has festered in his heart for many years. It is this secret that has turned him into the bitter man he is today, blaming everyone else in the world for his unhappiness."

Now my curiosity is growing into anxiety. Am I going to end up feeling sorry for him or will I dislike him even more than I do now? I fight the urge to bite my nails, something I have never done before. I take my hands and tuck them underneath my thighs.

"You see, your father lied to me about his efforts to keep my parents from being deported to a concentration camp. In Germany, your father was a junior reporter at one of the Berlin newspapers. He made friends with several Nazis, including a few that were Gestapo. When the rumors began that Jews were being taken away, your father started spending time at Gestapo headquarters, being chummy, drinking with them, and hoping to convince them that, even though he had a Jewish wife, he was in no way a sympathizer of the Jews. Of course, my parents and I did not think this was necessary, because we were German Jews - German first, Jewish second. They were born and raised in Berlin, as was I. Why, we had never even attended a service in a synagogue. We naively thought that what was happening would have nothing to do with us."

Tears start to fall from Mother's eyes. She turns her face away from me. She looks as if she is ashamed. "But to the Nazis, we were Jews first. Eventually, my parents lost their posts as music teachers at the Conservatory. Later, I was dismissed from the Ballet School where I was well on my way to becoming a principal dancer in the company.

"One day your father came home and told us that we could no longer go out into the streets. We were to stay indoors - indefinitely. For months my parents and I stood hiding behind the heavy drapes in our apartment, watching our friends, and neighbors being taken from their homes with only what they could carry, being made to march like cattle to somewhere unknown. When we could not bear this any longer, we pulled the drapes shut. In the meantime your father was coming home each day, telling us that it was just a matter of time till he would have papers for my parents to immigrate to Switzerland."

"So he did try?" I ask.

"Yes, he did but he was too naive to see what his so-called 'friends' really thought of him."

"What do you mean, Mother?"

"What your father never told me was that the Gestapo offered him a deal. My life, in exchange for my parents and any other Jews that he knew were in hiding. Of course, for him, there was no choice. It was me or them and he could not live without me. Unfortunately, in the end, it was all for nothing anyway. They took my parents and then came for me three months later, during the day, when your father was at work."

"But he should have been there to protect you, to fight them off, kill them if he had to! How come he didn't know?"

"He did know."

Mother gives me a minute to digest what she has just said. I am so shocked, I can't tell if I feel sick, angry, or disgusted. Mother goes on.

"One afternoon, two of his Gestapo friends called your father to come to headquarters. They had something to discuss with him. It was a ruse to distract him while I was being removed from our apartment. When he got to Gestapo headquarters, his friends told him they had no choice, they were sorry, but that his wife was being taken away at that very moment. Your father could not believe what they were saying. He thought it was a sick joke - that they were having their sadistic fun with him. The more terrified he got, the more they laughed. Your father went down on his knees and pleaded like a child for them to let me go. But that wasn't enough for the Gestapo. They wanted to humiliate him more. One of them mocked your father by asking him what made his Jewish wife so special. How wild was she in bed? They wanted details. He gave them answers he thought they wanted to hear. When it seemed like they had enough, they said he could leave. With the heels of their boots, they made your father crawl away on all fours. Once outside the headquarters, your father, hardly able to stand, managed to slowly pull himself up. Disoriented, he stood there, a broken man. And then, as if all the humiliation they put him through wasn't enough, one of the officers shouted out, "Joseph, just think of it this way, now there will be no chance of your Jewish whore of a wife bringing a Jewish child into our new Germany. I will make sure to recommend you for a commendation for your unselfish act of honor. Heil Hitler." Their howling laughter has haunted your father to this day, as did his lack of courage to kill himself.

"But if the Germans were so horrible, why does he hate the Jews so much?"

"Because everyone hates the Jews! Of course, it would have been easier for him if he did not love me so much. I was a Jew that kept him from the life he had imagined. And it was also his guilt that he could not let go of."

Mother's words make my heart ache. I can't catch my breath. I look at Mother. She is so calm, at peace, but I can't stay in this room with her another minute. I clench my fists. All I want to do is pound them into my father's face, over and over.

I run into my room, open the window wide, and gulp the cold air. Once I can breathe again, I reach under my bed and take out my sketchbooks. I search for the drawings I did of Father and rip each and every one of them into as many pieces as I can, letting them scatter around my feet.

"Michael, what are you doing?"

I hadn't heard Mother enter the room. Without moving or saying a word, I watch her as she circles around me, first staring at the torn up images lying around me, forming a puzzle of eyes, hair, chins, lips. She sits down on my bed and begins to look through the sketchpads spread out. My eyes are focused on her expressions as she goes through each drawing, every portrait. When she finishes, Mother looks up at me with wonder.

"Michael, I had no idea. They are beautiful."

"Well, as you said, you haven't been around a lot," I answer, wanting to hurt her.

"I deserve that," Mother says sadly.

I take the pads and whatever loose drawings there are and move them to the top of my desk, arranging them neatly. They are now out in the open. I'm not going to hide them anymore. I then tell her I am going to be an artist and not a violinist.

Lila

One Week After

He's home. I check the clock; it's twelve thirty at night. Another night of overtime. He heads for the kitchen. I've kept my door locked for five days, but I'm not mad anymore. I've been lonely without him and I miss him.

I get out of bed, brush my hair, pinch my cheeks, and spray just the teeniest bit of Lilac perfume behind my ears. I open the door to the living room and look to make sure Mom is not around. Daddy has told her never to wait up for him, that he does not want to see her and argue. But with her, you never know. I step quietly into the kitchen and watch him from the door for a moment. He's seated, smoking a cigarette, a glass of whiskey in front of him. He rubs his neck, trying to massage the tiredness away. I tiptoe up to him and put my hands gently over his eyes. He takes my hands and kisses them.

"I have missed you," he says with longing.

"I've missed you too. Sorry, I've been so awful."

"You never have to apologize to me," Daddy says.

He lets go of my hand and brings me around to him. I stand very still as his eyes linger on mine. "Go back to bed. Tomorrow I will finish at work early and pick you up after your voice lesson, and then we go for Chinese. Would you like that?"

"Yes, Daddy. I love you."

There are times when it's hard to tell what he's thinking. Girls my age should not be thinking the thoughts I have, but then again, I'm not like other girls my age. I never have been. I've always felt older. Daddy says I'm just very mature for my age and that's what makes me stand out.

I'm glad that it's all over now, and Daddy and I can go back to the way it was. I promise myself that I will stick to my New Year's resolution, which is to work as hard as I can to get into Performing Arts, where I will become the best at everything I do! Everyone will want to know me. And all the kids here at school and in this neighborhood will be green-eyed with envy, especially Sarah. Even Michael will be sorry that he wasn't nicer to me.

Sarah

One Week Later

The phone is ringing and no one's picked up yet. Well, I sure as hell am up now. With one eye open, I look at my alarm clock - it's seven-thirty. I've learned already that bad news always comes late at night or early in the morning but on a weekend, that's even worse so I better answer it.

Mom is already in the kitchen. She's smiling and waving her hand at me. This is good, no bad news. God knows I've had enough to deal with this week, worrying about Michael and his mother.

"Here she is. Now, don't be a stranger. You hear me," Mom says into the phone.

She hands me the phone and whispers Michael's name. My heart starts to thump! I can't believe it's him! I snatch the phone out of her hand.

"Jesus, where the hell have you been? A whole week's gone by. Why didn't you call? Are you OK? Is your Mother OK? God, I've been so worried. It's like you just disappeared. Are you angry with me? Did I do anything wrong?"

Silence on the other end. I repeat his name twice. I stare at the phone. Did he hang up on me? "Michael, say something!" I cry out.

"Sarah! Slow down. You're talking so fast, you're not giving me a chance to say anything. Can you meet me downstairs in an hour?"

"Of course, are you kidding? I'll be there with bells on!"

I get dressed in no time and scarf down breakfast. Just as I open the door, Mom calls out to me. "Sarah, please don't nudge him about New Year's, just listen. Maybe he will talk, maybe not, understand?"

"OK," I say and fly out the door.

The cold air knocks me for a loop. It's freezing out here! The stoop and steps have light crystals on them. I can jump up and down to keep warm or just sit my behind down, and grin and bear it. Even if my tush turns into a block of ice, it'll be worth it. I wrap my arms around me as tight as I can and wait.

When I think about New Year's Eve, I feel sad. I had hoped that Michael would stay over, but I knew he wouldn't leave his mother alone with his father. And after meeting Mr. Stein that night, I couldn't blame him. Michael's father is a very scary man. Dudley said that Mr. Stein made the hairs on his neck stand up! And Dad agreed with him. After Michael left, I went into my room and sat at the window, looking into his, hoping he would be there waiting for me, to let me know he was OK. But there was no sign of him. His shades were down, the lights out. I thought about calling but it was too late. Besides, I didn't want to think about what would happen if I did and Mr. Stein picked up.

I pulled up a chair, put my elbows on the window sill, and decided to wait. Mom came in a few minutes later and stood behind me, her hands on my shoulders.

"Mom, you think they're all right?"

"I hope so. I have such *rachmones* for Michael and his mother. Mr. Stein needs to learn that his wife and son don't want to be cut off from everyone, alone anymore. For his sake and theirs, I hope he does." Fat chance, I thought.

Now I'm sitting here on the stoop and my toes are starting to talk to me. I look down at my feet and see that I'm wearing my slippers. No wonder they're going numb. What if I get frostbite? I could lose my toes. Where are you, Michael? I rub and wriggle my toes back and forth but it doesn't help. Running out of ideas, I get up and start hopping from one foot to the other and pray that no one sees me, because I must look like I'm doing an Indian war dance. And what if I slip, break my feet and legs, and get rushed to the hospital and all before Michael even comes out! God, if he doesn't show up soon, my brain will probably get freezer burn, too. The hell with it, I am going to march over to his building and knock on his door. Not so easy. Each step I take, my slippers stick to the ice. Great, what now? Suddenly, I hear his laugh.

"Sarah, slippers? I swear you are the kookiest girl I know!"

"Michael, I'm the only girl, you know!"

It's been just a week since I've seen him but, if it's at all possible, he's more handsome than ever, but he seems different, older. Hmm, maybe that's what happens when you hit fourteen. He reaches out to me and hugs me.

"You good?" I ask.

"Yes, I am."

"What do you feel like doing? Do you want to go to the deli and have breakfast? Then we can sit and talk and you can tell me everything - if you want to?"

"First things first. You need to get some gloves, a scarf, a warmer coat, pants and boots," Michael says with great authority.

"Where're we going, the North Pole?"

"No, we are going ice skating!"

"You're kidding me, right? What about your hands? Your father will kill you if you get hurt."

"Don't worry, I'll be fine. Besides I'm not going to be playing the violin for a while. I have decided that I want to be an artist."

"Michael, you're putting me on, right?" I ask in disbelief.

He doesn't say a word, just shakes his head up and down and grins.

"And your parents are OK with this?"

"My Mother knows but not my father, not yet," Michael says softly.

There are a thousand questions I'm dying to ask him, but I remember Mom's words, "Don't nudge him. Just listen."

Something tells me that I should take her advice.

"Come on upstairs. You can talk to my mom while I change."

Michael is greeted by one of Mom's famous bear hugs - there is nothing better. When she's finished gushing over him, she notices how I'm dressed but, instead of getting angry, she only laughs. "Sarah, what am I going to do with you? It's winter and the temperature is thirty-two degrees. You're walking around like you are in Florida! Go, go, put on warm clothes and boots, please. Michael and I will sit here and have a cup of tea and some cookies. I just baked them. And, Sarah, woolen socks!"

When we're ready to leave, Mom stuffs our pockets with more cookies and two apples. "Ice skating will make you hungry. Go enjoy," Mom says.

Once we're outside, I playfully punch Michael. "We're really going ice skating?" I ask, still not convinced.

"Yes, Sarah, we are. It'll be fun! Besides, you're with me and you're going to make sure I don't fall or get hurt. I bet you're a wonderful skater."

"That I'm not so sure about. You put too much trust in me."

"I do," Michael says with enough sugar in his voice to fill a bowl.

After one hour, Michael is so at ease, I could swear that he was born wearing ice skates. Before I know it, he lets go of my hand and, without any fear, gracefully glides off on his own. Soon he's doing spins, and small leaps. Each time he lands on his feet, he giggles just like a little kid learning how to ride a bike. At some point, the other skaters have all stopped and are watching him, a vision of pure grace and beauty. Is there nothing he can't do? Someone starts to clap, and then others do the same. I skate up to him and take him by the hand and tell him to bow. Michael is surprised by the attention he's getting and looks at me, totally puzzled.

"Sarah, what's going on?"

"You. You're what's going on, silly. I thought you told me you never skated before,"

"I swear it's the first time. And it's amazing—skating makes me feel as if I can do anything."

"It sure looks like that," I say, adoringly. "Come on, my Prince Charming, how about we go for some pizza and you tell me what else you want to do in this world?"

It's snowing hard enough that, when we enter Gino's Pizza, we have to brush the snow from each other's hair and our clothes. Starving, we run to a booth in the back. The waitress takes our order for a large pie with everything on it and we settle in. We stare at each other, let out a deep breath as if we had just climbed the highest mountain, and then, suddenly, we both fall silent. For me, an overwhelming feeling of calmness fills me. I look into Michael's eyes to see if he's feeling the same as me, but he looks far away.

"You OK?" I ask.

"I'm better than OK. I'm really, really happy. Thank you, Sarah, for being my friend."

As touching and sweet as his words are, I feel sad and happy at the same time. I wish he would feel more for me. But I realize with each day that a friend is all I will ever be to him. I'll just have to settle for that, because Michael Stein is always going to be a part of my life.

Michael

Michael Tells Maestro And Confides In Tommy

Maestro is so shocked by my announcement that he starts frantically tapping his chest as if he's about to have a heart attack. I expected him to be upset but not like this. I have to get Signora; she'll know what to do. But as soon as I get up, Maestro beats me to it as he calls out for her. "Mamma Mia! Gabriella, *vieni qui, presto*!"

Signora rushes in. Her eyes dart from me to him. Maestro groans. She asks, "*che cosa*?"

"Gabriella, you will not believe what Michael just say to me! I cannot even repeat the words. They are like a knife to my heart!" Maestro waves his hand in the air, first pointing at me and then at his wife. He wants me to tell her. I clear my throat.

"Signora, I've decided that I do not want to be a violinist. I want to be an artist."

Maestro gives out a heavy sigh. Signora slaps the Maestro on the forehead. "*Dai, Dai*, Giorgio, *per favore*."

Signora turns to me, cups my face in her hands.

"Michael, you sure?" she asks.

"Signora, I have been thinking about this for a long time. I will always have music in my life, but not as a concert violinist."

"You have told your parents?"

"My mother, yes. She said I should follow my heart. My father, no. He will not be happy."

"Sit, Michael, please," says Signora.

Meanwhile, Maestro slowly gets up from his chair and picks up my violin. Holding it close to him, like you would a baby, he gently places the violin in its case as if it is a coffin. The sound of the clasp locking gives me a jolt and surprisingly, a feeling of sadness and then freedom. Suddenly a bright red handkerchief appears in the Maestro's hand. With a dramatic grand gesture, he waves it in the air and drapes it over the violin case. Signora walks up to the Maestro, takes the handkerchief from his hands and puts it in her apron pocket.

"*Dio mio*! This is not a death. Please. Enough," begs Signora. "Giovanni, wish the boy good luck."

Maestro turns to me, looks into my eyes, and puts his hand on my shoulders. "Michael, *Scusa.* My wife is right. I wish you nothing but happiness. Most important is to love what you do. *Per favore,* do not be a stranger. You come visit us. And you make sure you bring your work for us to see."

Maestro takes my hands, holds them out, and puts his lips to them. "Michael, these hands have the gift of extraordinary talent. I have no doubt they will serve you well." With that, Maestro leaves the room, his body weighed down by my decision.

I will miss this room and these two wonderful people. For a long time, they have been my only friends. Signora walks me to the door, takes my face in her hands, and kisses me on both cheeks. I inhale her familiar scent of flour, sugar, and dark coffee. For a moment I want to stay and sit a while longer, but, at the same time, I suddenly have a huge craving for something sweet, filled with chocolate and whipped cream. I don't have to think twice where I'm heading.

Several blocks later, I'm standing across the street from Tommy's father's bakery. From here I can see Tommy behind the counter, talking it up to the customers. He makes it look so easy. Tommy makes people laugh, especially the women. It doesn't matter if they are young or old. Tommy DeMarco flirts with them all. Everyone walks out with a smile. I'd like to go in, say hello, and buy something, but I'm still feeling shy around him. Better if I just sit on the bench and watch.

The bakery is busy. After about a half hour, there are only two people left, a man and a girl. They're both pointing at the glass cases filled with pastries. Tommy takes out the ones they choose and puts them in a cake box. He says something to the girl. She turns away from him, walks to the front door, and waits for the man to finish paying at the cash register. When they come out of the bakery, I take a second look. It's Lila and her father. They walk to the corner and Mr. Rosen, looking annoyed, stops and whispers something to Lila. Whatever he's said to her has made her upset. Lila quickly turns away from him and starts to cross the street. To her surprise, she sees me right away. From the expression on her face, she knows that I've been watching them and she looks upset.

Embarrassed, I look away as if she's not there. That's when I notice Tommy standing outside the bakery. He's been watching Lila, too. He sees me and now the two of them are staring at me. Oh, God, I bet they think I'm some kind of creep.

I hear Mr. Rosen's voice and, before I know it, Lila has gone back to her father. They turn around the corner and are gone. Now it's only Tommy looking at me. He takes out a cigarette from his T-shirt pocket, lights it, and blows smoke rings into the air. Since I don't know what else to do, I wave at him.

"Hey, genius, what are you doing over there?" Tommy shouts.

I shrug my shoulders, put my hand to my ear, and pretend I can't hear him. He makes the next move by crossing the street and sitting down next to me. He spreads his arms out on the back of the bench, looks around, and offers me his cigarette.

"Finished your violin lesson early today?"

"I didn't take a lesson today."

"Yeah, I bet sometimes you just get tired. Hey, you want a drag?"

"Nah, not right now," I say trying to sound all natural like.

Tommy breaks out laughing. "Who you kidding? You don't smoke."

"No, I don't."

"Hey, to tell you the truth, I'm not all that crazy about it. But it makes you look cool with the other guys . . . and the girls, too. You know what I mean?"

I can't believe he just told me this. Could this mean we're becoming friends? I guess he notices the puzzled look on my face because he laughs again and looks me straight in the eye. "Hey, it's not like I'm following you or anything . . . it's just that a day don't go by when the Maestro don't come in after a lesson with you and praise the hell out of you to my Pop and me. He calls you a genius. That's why I called you that. So he ain't shown up yet and you did, so I put two and two together," Tommy says proudly.

"I didn't take a lesson today because I needed to tell him something."

"Sounds serious," Tommy says, looking at me with curiosity.

"It was," I answer, unsure of whether I should tell him or not.

Tommy gives me a wink like it's OK. We sit quietly as if we've been friends for years. He finishes his cigarette and starts to go.

"Hey, you want to know what I told him?" I ask, surprising myself.

"Sure, why not."

"I told him that I'm giving up the violin. I'm going to be an artist."

"For real? Ub*atz*! What your parents say?"

"My mother is fine with it. The Maestro is going to need some time, but he wishes me luck. I haven't told my father."

"Hell, if it was my pop, he'd kill me. All those years of lessons, money . . . shit, you got *avere i coglioni*, *capeesh!*" Michael says, holding on to his crotch.

I start to laugh, soon the two of us are cracking up. I wish this moment would never end. But in a second it does; Mr. DeMarco is shouting to Tommy from across the street.

Tommy signals his dad he's coming back. "I gotta go. But

you stand up to your old man, OK?"

He gives me thumbs up and a smile that stirs up my insides.

February

Sarah

Caught By Surprise

At assembly this morning, Mr. Doran spoke to us about our entering high school in the fall and the new voyage we will be embarking on. Well, I've already decided where my voyage is taking me—120 West 45th St., The High School of Performing Arts in Manhattan. And after school today I'm meeting with Miss Prescott, my English teacher, to read the two one-minute monologues she chose for me. One is Mary from *The Children's Hour* by Lillian Hellman and the other is Frankie from *The Member of the Wedding* by Carson McCullers. When I first announced to Miss Prescott that I wanted to audition for Performing Arts, her reaction was way more positive than I expected.

"Oh, Sarah, that's wonderful. You have the magic it takes to transform yourself into anyone and make it believable. I will be very happy to help you and the other girls who are auditioning, too. I am very proud of all of you."

She tells me, "There are three others besides you - Judy, Renee, and Arlene." Two of them I like and the third I don't really know. Arlene is very pretty—shy, a little mysterious. It's possible that she could be my strongest competition. But I'm not worried." Oh, I almost forgot, there will be one more. Lila Rosen will also be trying out for the Drama Department," says Miss Prescott, with pride.

Shit! No! I can't believe it.

"Miss Prescott, can she do that? I mean try out for both dance and drama?"

"Yes, not many do. There is a tremendous amount of work involved, plus having to keep up one's grades. At first, I was not so sure about her decision. I had Mr. Rosen come in and we had a long talk. He was very convincing of Lila's ability to handlc what was required by the school. He seems to have her future all planned out." Miss Prescott hesitates for a second . . . "I just hope for Lila's sake that . . . well, never mind."

Never mind is right. I mean, it's not like I didn't know that she was going to be trying out for the school. Max and Lila have been talking and preparing for years. But it was always just for dance. Now, if both of us get in, it means we'll be on the train together, seeing each other every day in the hallways, probably sharing some classes. God, I can't bear to think about it.

When I complain to Michael, he says I'm worrying too much. "You'll barely see each other. Your schedules will be totally different."

Easy for him to say. As much as he listens to me, he really can't truly understand how Lila can creep into my head and make me shrink with fear or fill me with guilt. What drives me nuts, though, is that no one can imagine just how evil Lila is. I know for a fact that, if she has a choice, she'll pick the Drama Department over dance, just to spite me. If that happens, I'm not sure I want to go.

Lila

Feeling Doubtful

I wasn't too happy today when Miss Prescott announced that there would be seven of us auditioning for Performing Arts in March. Five for the Drama Department—other than Sarah, the only one I was surprised about was Arlene, a mousy little girl who has hardly said one word in class since she moved here three years ago, and three girls besides me for the Dance Department. I'm the only one auditioning for both. I'm not worried about the others; there is no competition except for maybe Sarah. Besides her being so super dramatic about everything, Sarah does have something that makes her stand out. Of course I'd never tell her that. Anyway, I'm hoping that her hatred for me will be greater than her ambition and that the thought of spending another four years with me will make her bow out. I can also try to come up with something awful to do to her, and then she'd have no choice. But that would take too much time away from me working as hard as I can towards my goals. If I do get accepted by both the Dance and Drama Departments, then I'll be noticed by all the teachers and looked up to by the other students. I'd like that. Maybe I'll even make friends. But that will only happen if Sarah doesn't get accepted.

I hope Daddy comes in to say goodnight. I want to talk to

him about Sarah trying out and how that makes me nervous. But he's been arguing with Mom for the last hour. I can't hear what it's about, but I'm sure it's got something to do with the money that is being spent for the extra acting lessons he's signed me up for. Mom thinks that I'm not worth it, that I'm not who he thinks I am. Deep down inside I have my doubts, too. What if she's right? My teachers tell me I'm talented, and hardworking, and that my beauty will take me far. But I never get the feeling that they see me in the special way that Daddy does.

Their voices have lowered. The front door opens and closes. He's gone. When he and Mom have a fight, he leaves and goes for long walks, sometimes late into the night. But he always comes back to me.

It must have been raining outside, because Daddy's head is resting next to mine, and I feel the dampness in his hair, and smell the whiskey on his breath. I don't even have to open my eyes to know that his are already closed.

"What were you and Mom arguing about?" I whisper to him.

"Nothing for you to worry about. You just concentrate on your lessons and getting into that school and I will take care of your mother."

He nuzzles in closer. His breathing becomes faint and he starts to snore lightly. When I wake up in the morning, he will be gone from my bed.

Sarah

Sarah Loses Heart

I've been sitting in the library since classes ended. It's now three-thirty, and my reading for Miss Prescott is at four. A whole thirty minutes to go. I can continue to hang out here and keep going over the monologues or just walk over to the classroom and wait there. I'm a bit more than nervous. Today is the first time I'll be reading to her. And I want it to be perfect, if not outright amazing! What the hell, I'm going.

The door to Miss Prescott's classroom is closed, but I hear a voice. Probably one of the other girls auditioning for Performing Arts is reading also. I wonder who's in there. I look around to make sure no one else is around. It wouldn't look right if they saw me with my ear plastered to the door. I turn left and right; the hallway is clear. I listen as carefully as I can and I recognize the voice right away. It's Lila reading the part of Mary in *The Children's Hour* - my Mary, my monologue. I can't believe it. It's such a shock—my blood is boiling! What the hell was Miss Prescott thinking?

The queasiness in my stomach is traveling up to my throat. I'm going to be sick. I try to hold it back but I can't. Shit . . . here it comes, oh no! Vomit all over. I feel gross and mortified. Don't know what's worse - my throwing up right outside the classroom door or the discovery that Lila has stolen something from me again. I have to get out of here; I can't let her see me.

After running for a few blocks, I stop and hide in the nearest alleyway. Standing under a half torn awning, garbage cans all around me, I bend my head towards my knees and try to catch my breath. All at once the skies open up and giant drops of rain come down on me. By the time I reach my building I am thoroughly drenched, but at least the smell of vomit has washed away.

Not wanting to talk to Mom, I sneak into the apartment quietly and go to my room. Without waiting a second, I swiftly peel off my wet clothes, crumble them up, stuff them into a pillowcase, and throw them into the back of my closet. Before running into the bathroom to shower, I take an old shirt and wipe up the wet footprints on the living room floor.

Mom is waiting for me when I come out of my bedroom.

"So, how did your reading go?"

I had made up my mind not to say anything to her, thinking she would say I was making a mountain out of a molehill, but I can't hold back anymore. In seconds, the words come spilling out like a waterfall. Mom rocks me gently in her arms as I tell her everything that happened. She listens carefully and suggests that I should get some rest.

"Right now you are shivering . . . I don't want you to get sick. I am sure it is a misunderstanding," Mom says, trying to make me feel better. "You sit down while I make some hot tea."

She puts a blanket over me, tucking me in like a baby. I've finally stopped crying and wait for her to come back. Suddenly I break out into a cold sweat and pray I'm wrong. I throw my blanket off and jump from the couch and run into my room. I make a dive for my backpack. My playbooks are missing! I had to have dropped them outside of Miss Prescott's classroom next to my puddle of shame.

Lila

Lila's Day Turns From Good To Bad

"Lila, please stop for a moment. Do you hear that?"

"Hear what, Miss Prescott?"

I put the monologue down and watch her opening the door.

"Oh, Lord, what in heaven?" she says. "Stay here, Lila, please."

In an instant, Miss Prescott is out of sight, but I hear her heels clacking loudly down the hallway, and she's shouting out Sarah's name. What the hell is going on?

There's no way I can just sit here. I step outside the classroom and the most awful smell stops me dead in my tracks. Holding my nose, I look down and stare at a . . . a gop of vomit. Totally disgusting! I carefully step over it and stand in the middle of the hallway trying to see where Miss Prescott is. When she calls out Sarah's name again, she's no longer shouting. Her voice sounds sad. I rush back into the room and look out the window. I can just about make out the back of Sarah's head, her ponytail bobbing high into the air like a kite, as she runs down the steps of the school.

Meanwhile, there is this slime to be cleaned up. I definitely don't want to be the one to do it, but I should at least look like I'm trying. I get a bunch of paper towels from the closet and step outside. I kneel down, swearing under my breath, and notice something out of the corner of my eye. Just inches away are two play books on the floor. I stretch my hand out and reach for them. This is too good to be true. One of them is *The Children's Hour*, and the page is turned to the same monologue I am reading.

I flip the pages and see Sarah's notes written all over it. She must have been outside the door listening to me and freaked out. There was no way for her to know that I was going to read Mary's monologue or even that I picked it. Miss Prescott had chosen the same play for me but for the part of Rosalie, the good girl in the play.

"There is such a natural sweetness and innocence about you, Lila. I think this is the right character for you."

That's exactly what she said to me when she gave me the play. But I don't like Rosalie; she's too dull. Mary is definitely more me, but I will never let Miss Prescott know that. So this morning I decided to read Mary instead. I told Miss Prescott I wanted more of a challenge. She was impressed with that.

The sound of Miss Prescott's heels clicking tells me she's coming back. I quickly hide the books under the band in my skirt and start to energetically wipe the floor. In a matter of seconds, Miss Prescott appears in front of me. She bends down, takes my hand, and lifts me up.

"Lila, you do not have to do this. I will take care of it. I have to say, I really don't know what to make of all this. You can go home now," she says, sounding perplexed.

I try to look as upset as her and ask if there is anything that I can do. But she's not even paying attention to me now, so I go, which I'm not unhappy about. All the way home, I hold on tightly to my waist to make sure my hidden secret does not slip out. I'm getting more excited by the minute. I can't wait to see Sarah's face when I return the plays to her.

As soon as Hannah opens the door, it's obvious that I'm not welcome, I hear Sarah in the background, whispering to her mother.

"Hi, Hannah, is Sarah OK? I heard she got sick in school so I just came by to see how she is," sounding as sincere as possible.

"A little stomach bug, that's all. Some chicken soup, hot tea, and she will be fine. I will tell her you dropped by. Thank you. Lila."

The door closes. I knock again. Hannah opens.

"What is it, Lila?"

I hand her the two plays. "I almost forgot. Sarah dropped these outside of Miss Prescott's classroom. I know she needs them."

I would love to see her face, it would be so sweet. But knowing that right now she's raving mad is good enough for me . . . until I realize I'm standing here in the hallway, feeling a little lost. Should I go home and do homework? Call it a day or leave and see if I can find something out there to entertain me? I might as well go home. As I walk towards my apartment, the odor of Mom's cabbage soup and mystery meat comes right out into the hallway, where in just seconds it will spread like fire into the hallways of each floor of the building. My mind is made up. I'm out of here.

I've been at Harry's for a half an hour. I've had my egg cream. Went through all the movie magazines. No one has walked in since I got here. Dull, dull, dull!

"Lila, sweetheart, time to go, I gotta close up," says Harry.

"Harry, what are you having for dinner tonight?"

He looks at me with sad and knowing eyes. "Your momma making that goulash again?"

"Yup, it's my lucky night," I answer with sarcasm.

"Sorry, kid, wish I could help you. Go pick out a chocolate for after. It's on me."

I walk up to Harry and give him a peck on the cheek. He blushes.

"No, thanks, Hollywood doesn't like fat girls," I say playfully. I turn and walk out the door and, BOOM, I bump right into Tommy DeMarco.

"Well, well, look who's here," he says.

Oh, my God, here's the guy that everyone thinks is the coolest and toughest guy in the neighborhood, and he can hardly look me straight in the eye. He's also blushing, which is kind of cute. Well, maybe today won't be such a bust. Teasing him will be fun. I lower my eyelashes and then, ever so slowly, I bite down on my lip just enough to drive him crazy. I've practiced this expression a hundred times and it always gets the boys all hot and bothered.

Tommy is just about to say something when a screeching voice yells out his name. He snaps his head around. Across the street, BoBo screams his name. She is looking so pissed off that I would not be surprised if flames came shooting out from her nostrils. I start to ask Tommy if she's always like this, when I see that his eyes are begging me not to say anything.

"Shit, she don't like you. Sorry babe, I gotta go."

"TOMMY DEMARCO," BoBo yells out again.

Unbelievable. The guy is truly afraid of her. I want to laugh but don't dare. The last thing I need is to make him look like a wimp, and he's not worth getting me on BoBo's shit list. Time to go home.

Tommy runs his hands through his thick beautiful head of black hair, shrugs his shoulders, and crosses the street to BoBo. She says something to him and links her arm with his. The two of them walk away, but BoBo takes a second to turn and stare at me. Oh, I will have to stay away from her.

Coming out of the elevator, I have to pinch my nose for the second time today and hold my breath. God, I hate that smell. I swear, when Daddy and I leave here. I will never, ever, eat that garbage again. Quiet as a mouse, I go into the apartment and pray that Mom does not hear me. All I want to do is open the window, stick my head out, and avoid getting sick. But, no luck. The door to my bedroom is open.

Mom is sitting on my bed. Her knees and feet are spread apart; her hands are at her sides and curled into fists. She's got the look of a wrestler who's about to pounce on his opponent, which in this case is me.

"What are you doing in my room?" I ask.

Mom slowly releases one fist and dangles a thin gold chain with a gold heart. Where you steal this from?"

"I didn't steal it. It was a present!"

She cups the necklace in her hands and holds it up close to her eyes. "And vat did you do to get a pretty trinket like this?"

It's no big secret that Mom thinks I'm a tramp. She'd like nothing better than for it to be true and right now she thinks she's proven it. But, for some reason, today her snide remark stings. Maybe it's because the whole day has been a bust, or the disgusting food that she'll make me eat later, or the fact that she's been in my room snooping about, but, whatever it is, I'm done! Before she can say anything else, I snatch the necklace from her hand and put it around my neck.

"If you really want to know, it was Daddy," I say, sounding as wicked as I can.

Even after all these years, I'm still surprised to see how much she hates me.

Mom lifts her heavy body from the bed and from behind her back she reaches out for her trusty rolled-up magazine. I prepare myself for what's coming next by stiffening my shoulders, sucking in my cheeks, and pressing my lips together as tight as I can. I stare back at her with as much hate as she has for me and wait. Before I can count to ten, she whacks me, one . . . two, three times on my behind. Hard! But today, it's not enough for her. She drops the magazine and raises her hand towards my face. But I'm a hell of a lot faster than her and catch her by the wrist. I dig my fingernails into her palm. The unspoken rule has always been - never my face! If Daddy ever saw a mark, there would be no place for her to hide.

I let go and Mom's body collapses like a large deflated balloon. In no time, the embarrassing blotches break out on her face and the awful scratching begins. To my surprise, I'm suddenly feeling sorry for her. I leave and go into the bathroom. I take a washcloth and run warm water over it. When I come back, Mom is scratching away and the blotches have spread to her arms. I take the towel and gently blot her face. But instead of being thankful, she takes the washcloth, throws it on the floor and storms out of my room. She slams the door.

Her rejection feels like I've been punched in the stomach. Cramps start to take hold. I drop to the floor and rock myself back and forth. After a few minutes, I need to go to the bathroom. I sit on the toilet and pull down my underpants. Shit, it's blood and it's repulsive. I've gotten the curse. My God, what else can possibly happen to make this day any worse?

Sarah

Present From Michael

Mom comes into the room and whips my blanket off me. "Come on, get up. Enough with the sulking. Michael called; he's coming over. Get washed and dressed and be ready in one hour. Also, he says to look out your window."

Mom pulls the window shade up with such force that it makes a sharp snapping sound. I cover my head, afraid that it's going to let loose from the bar it's on and come flying at me. When she closes the door with a loud bang, I know she means business.

I really freaked out after hearing Lila read my monologue last week. I was in such a major funk and depression that at times I scared myself. Mom got so worried that she let me stay home from school for a few days. At first she believed I really did have a stomach bug, but then she got wise. And now I think she's had it with me. I wanted to tell Mom how much I hate Lila for always coming out shining, that she will always win, and that she will always be better than me, but I was too ashamed.

Michael and Roxy think I'm obsessed with Lila. Maybe I am. But I can't help it. For better or worse, so many of my insecurities, frustrations, and thousands of evil thoughts that run through my head are because of her. I get out of bed and look out at Michael's window. There is a sign that fills the whole bottom half. Large red hearts surround the words: I LOVE YOU AND MISS YOU!

Seeing Michael makes me feel all warm and tingly. He gives me a huge hug and then looks at me seriously. "Here, this is for you," Michael says, handing me a box with a red ribbon.

"What's this?" I ask.

"Sarah, just open it and take a minute before you say anything."

I untie the ribbon, take the cover off and make a face. "Michael, you know I hate diaries."

"Don't be a spoiled brat, look at the cover . . . it says journal, not diary. A journal is the grown-up version. Honestly, Sarah, you can't walk around all the time so angry."

"You're exaggerating . . . I am a very happy person."

"Not lately, you're not. And, I know what happened last week. Or I think I do. Lila told me her side of the story."

"Which I am sure is very different from mine," I answer, fuming. I throw the journal aside, cross my arms, and give Michael a fixed stare.

"Ok, so what's yours?"

I turn my back to Michael because I don't want him to see I'm about to cry.

"That's not going to help. And giving me and everyone else around you the silent treatment is getting boring," he adds.

I'm surprised to hear Michael talk to me this way. I've never known him to be so bold. I am hurt. Tears start gushing down my face. Michael touches me on the shoulder and turns me around. His long arms wrap around me. "Sarah, you have to let go. I swear. If you write down your feelings, you will be surprised at how much it will help. I swear!"

I let Michael hold me for a while, then I pick up the journal and brush my fingers across the red leather cover: "Journal" is embossed in gold letters. Inside, the pages are thick and a beautiful creamy beige. This doesn't look or feel at all like a diary. Most are designed for young girls who have only sweet thoughts: the kind where every first event, medal, dance, kiss, and heartbreak are recorded. Pages get filled with doodles, colored hearts, pressed flowers, a first corsage. Roxy has had one since the fourth grade and writes in it every night. She let me look at it once and it made me depressed. Not because she wrote about unhappy things, but because everything in it was so sugary and innocent. Everything I'm not.

I start to tell Michael about what happened with Lila. He takes my hand. "Don't tell me, write it down. Get it all out here," he says, pointing to the pages.

"But why can't I tell you these things. You're my best friend."

"One, you don't always tell me. Two, it's not always that easy. Sometimes we're so afraid that, if people know what we really think, they won't love us anymore. Some secrets go too deep. I know that. Trust me."

Michael gently takes the journal from my hand and with a pen starts to write something on the first few pages. When he's finished, he hands it back to me.

"Read this every day when you get up, anytime when you think you're going to lose it, and every night before you close your eyes."

I close the journal without looking at what he wrote.

"Listen, Sarah, if you want to get into Performing Arts, you have to concentrate. It's not an easy school to get into. But you can do it. You just have to stop wasting your time being upset by Lila. I'm telling you all this because you have to start feeling better about yourself."

"Michael, maybe you're right, but I don't have to concentrate on getting into Performing Arts anymore. I've made up my mind. I'm not going to audition," I say this as a declaration.

Michael's jaw drops and he stares at me with a look of frustration.

"Ok, give me one good reason why and it better be a good one."

I hesitate but I've given this a lot of thought. “It's simple. Lila is very good. She'll get in and I won't." He looks at me with such disappointment that I want to hide.

I'm afraid to tell him that, if I spill my deepest thoughts on paper, then even I won't like myself. I've too many bad ones. Like the one where I wish that someone would kidnap Lila and she'd never be found. Or that Fritzy gets a horrible infection that causes her tongue to fall out. This way she wouldn't be able to spread all the lies that she does.

Roxy told me a while back that she heard Fritzy tell her mom terrible things about Dudley and Mom. Like, how low can Fritzy get? When I saw Lila, I asked her if she knew anything about it and she just snickered.

"Listen, Sarah, we all know that my mom is crazy jealous of your mother. And you of all people should know about being jealous, right? But, other people are . . . noticing things too."

"Like what?"

"Oh like Dudley hanging around more than usual with your mom and Mrs. Stein. I mean, you'd think they were the three musketeers," Lila says with a wicked grin. Her words were as sharp as needles and they hurt. I couldn't say a word. I just walked away.

I thought about telling Mom what Lila said but decided not to. It would break Mom's heart. And she sure as hell would be furious with Fritzy. God knows what Mom would do to her. So it's that kind of stuff that makes me have unspeakable thoughts. But what would really scare me the most is if I did write down my darkest thoughts and then have an accident and die and Mom found the journal. Once she read it, she'd discover how cruel and evil I was. It would kill her. She'd never forgive me. Never! And the very worst thing that could ever happen is that Lila shows up after my funeral and takes my place as her daughter. This is when my fantasies turn into nightmares. Suddenly, I feel a pinch on my hand.

"Sarah, hello! Earth to Sarah!"

"Ouch," I cry out. "What's that for?"

"You spaced out for a second. Listen to me. There is no way I'm going to let you quit. You're going to keep this journal, and you're going to rehearse and audition for Performing Arts. I'll work with you."

I open the journal and stare at the words Michael has written: "I am good, I am kind; I am smart, I am beautiful; I will no longer doubt myself and I will get into Performing Arts because I will knock them dead!"

For the first time in a long time, I feel my self-confidence start to boost up. I ask Michael to go into the living room and wait for me. I go into the bathroom, wash my face, put on a little powder, and lipstick, loosen my hair from my ponytail and whip my hair around.

When I come into the living room, Michael stares at me as if he is seeing someone else. I sit down on the couch across from him, cross my legs, put my hands gracefully on my lap, and smile.

Michael gets up from the chair, stands back, lifts his hands mid-air and swirls them around like he is about to perform a magic trick. I look at him like he's crazy, but then he totally surprises me by arranging his hands so it looks like he's holding a movie camera. First, he zooms in real close to me and slowly backs away saying, "Lights, camera, action!"

Michael

Time To Tell Father

By now pretty much everyone knows I'm applying to Music and Art except Father. When I stopped by the bakery today, Tommy asked me if told him yet, and I had to admit that I hadn't.

"I don't blame you. Shit, I'd be scared, too, but just remember - the longer you wait, the longer you lie to him, there's no knowing how he's gonna take it. But you can bet it ain't gonna be good. Know what I mean?"

Tommy is right; I've been thinking the same thing the last few days and dreading the idea of waiting. But I don't want Tommy to see my fear. "I can handle it. Besides it's not his life, it's mine," I answer, sounding confident.

"Ok, just stay cool," and Tommy walks away, scratching his head and grinning.

For some reason, by the time I get home, I'm not feeling as high and mighty as I did with Tommy. I walk into the kitchen and there's Mother at the stove. The radio is on, and she's swaying and humming to Franks Sinatra's "All the Way." I don't want to stop her. I like watching her, but we have to talk. The longer we keep our secret from him, the harder it will be for him to accept what we did.

"What, darling? You look like you have something on your

mind."

"We should tell him," I say.

"No, Michael. We wait as we planned. Trust me."

I know Mother is going out of her way to make sure that, when we get the news from Music and Art, Father will somehow be more open to listen to me about my decision and at the same time will be proud enough to not want to kill us.

Each day Mother does something extra to please Father and gives him little reason to get upset about anything. She makes special meals and bakes his favorite desserts. His newspapers (he reads at least four after supper each night) are always waiting for him next to his club chair. Sometimes, there's an unexpected show of affection - a hug, kiss, or a compliment for how handsome and smart he is. And then there's her new-found energy that bounces off the walls of the apartment and makes him smile. But every once in a while, I catch Father staring at her as if she is a stranger. And if she is, then who is he?

Deep inside I believe that whatever the outcome if I get into Music and Art or not, Mother and I have done the unthinkable . . . disobeyed his commands. We have disrespected him and, knowing this, he will always wonder what else we have kept from him. Mother swears that he is a changed man, but I am not so optimistic.

The one thing I know for sure is that I have changed, and, if there are consequences to follow, Father will learn quickly that he cannot take it out on Mother and that he can never raise a hand to her or me again. I won't let him.

March

Lila

Audition Day

The smell of Vicks Vapor Rub and the sound of her sickly wheezing cough wake me up. I roll over in bed, reach for my table lamp, and switch the light on. Mom is sitting in a chair against the door with her hands crossed high over her chest, staring at me with her usual sour look.

"Mom, how long have you been here in the dark?"

"So peaceful you and your daddy sleep, like babies. All week, I think how you and he have to be on pins and needles, but, no, both of you are always so sure of everything. That must feel good. Me, I never have that."

OK, Mom is giving me the creeps. I rub my eyes and take a look at my alarm clock. Jesus, it's three in the morning. At ten I'm going to be auditioning for Drama and Dance. I will be at the school for the whole day. I need my rest. What is she doing here?

"Something wrong? Is it your cold?"

"You are worried about me? Ah, so sweet of you to think of me when you have so much on your mind. Such a big day for you and Daddy."

"Is . . . he OK?"

"Yes. I told you, he sleeps like a baby."

"Great, so you want to tell me what you're doing here?"

Mom gets up from the chair and walks over to my bed. She looks down at me and then does something so unlike her that I flinch. Her blotched hand comes toward me and with her puffed up finger she strokes my head gently as if she really cares about me. I can't remember the last time that happened, if ever.

"I just want to wish you good luck but, also, give you a little advice."

"What?" I ask.

Mom cups my chin in her hand raises it up to hers and squeezes hard. The tenderness from a second ago is gone. "Be careful what you wish for, Lila. It may not always make you happy."

With a twisted smile, she pinches my chin again, this time harder, and then let's go. She turns my lamp off and leaves. Right away, like a crazy person, I start fanning my hands in the air, hoping to get rid of the stink from the Vicks. I yank my blanket over my head and try to go back to sleep.

But it's not working. Mom's good wishes, which sounded more like a curse, keep buzzing around in my ear. Oh no! My skin is starting to itch. I swear - if I get one hive, I'm going to kill her.

Daddy and I arrive at the school. Even though I got only a few hours sleep, I don't feel bad. Daddy says I look beautiful. He tells me not to worry about anything. "You will be wonderful and you will dazzle them," he says with great assuredness.

I leave him sitting on a bench in the hallway of the school along with the other parents. Before reaching the top of the stairs, I stop and turn to look at him one more time. He winks at me and gives me his "just for you smile," making me feel tingly. I quickly spin around and walk up the stairs to look for the drama studio, my first audition. OK. Breathe. Inhale, exhale, inhale, exhale. Head up. Never look at the floor. Make eye contact. Inhale, exhale.

I focus and smile directly at each of the two men and three women and introduce myself. But, as soon as I say my name, my tongue feels instantly weird, as if it's coated with glue. What's going on? Then like a mirage, Mom's face appears in front of me and she's laughing. The image of her scares me so much that I start to cough uncontrollably. My God, I'm unbelievably mortified. One of the teachers rushes up to me with a glass of water. They ask if I need to sit down. I shake my head no, take a minute to get myself together, and ask if I may continue. Looks are exchanged among the teachers as they hesitate for a minute, then tell me to begin.

Breathe, inhale, exhale. Whatever happens, I can't panic.

Mom's face fades. Somehow I get through the improvisational exercise and my two monologues. When it's over, I'm not sure who is more embarrassed, me or them. They thank me for coming and, with my head down, unable to look them in the eye, I say goodbye.

I run straight for the bathroom, find a stall and throw up. I feel light- headed; I splash cold water over my face and neck. Staring in the mirror, I'm amazed that I look normal, that it's me. Back in that audition room, I was someone else.

A group of girls enter the bathroom. They are all talking about their auditions. Some are laughing and some say nothing. One girl is beside herself and can't stop crying about how awful she was. I could make her feel better by telling her that, no matter how bad she thinks her audition went, it couldn't have been worse than mine. But I don't care; I just have to get out of here. My next audition is in one hour. I can go down and have Daddy reassure me that I'm OK, but then I would have to tell him what happened and I don't have the nerve.

The dance studio is on the top floor of the school. A tall, dark Negro boy in dance tights and a T-shirt stands by the door. "Hey, you don't look so good. Are you all right? My name is Spencer."

His voice is soft and sincere. Yet I am uncomfortable. Besides Dudley, who is loved by everyone in the neighborhood, I'm not used to being around colored people. "I'm fine, thank you."

"Well, the dressing room is to your right, the studio to your left. Good luck."

In the dressing room there are five other girls getting into their dance clothes. Trying not to be obvious, I sneak a look at my competition. Right away I regain my confidence. They are all pretty but not as pretty as me.

I change into my black leotard and tights and take out my ballet shoes. As soon as I slip my feet into them, I know something is wrong. I look down at them and see that they are not the shoes I packed in my bag last night. They look like mine but feel one size too small. I lunge into my dance bag and take out everything. It's all there, except for the right ballet shoes. Suddenly I can't breathe; I put my head down between my knees. This can't be happening. My toes are already cramping and I haven't danced one step. I don't know whether to scream or cry when, in a flash, it hits me, Mom did this. She only wants me to fail. Well, too bad because that's not going to happen. Determined not to let Mom win, I stand up, adjust my toes as best I can, and promise myself that, if I get through this today, she will pay.

The other girls and I line up and walk into the dance studio. I place myself last in line, just as Daddy instructed me to do. "Remember, you always save the best for last, and you, Lila, are the best!" In Daddy's mind, that's how he sees me and thinks everyone else will, too.

There are three dance masters, a piano accompanist, and two dance students standing off to the side. One of them is Spencer. He smiles at me as if we are old friends. The music starts and the audition begins.

The ballet and modern dance class were easy. Even with my aching toes, I managed to get through the pliés, assemblé, arabesque, dégagé with skill and grace, worthy of being a student at Performing Arts - I'm proud.

I have a few minutes to relieve my toes before I do my solo. I use the time to massage each of them and try to stretch my shoe. When my name is called out, I am as ready as I can be. I stand in the center of the Dance Studio and know that this is the moment. Waiting for my music to start, I lower my head. This is for you, Mom!

I perform the solo using every bit of willpower I have. Nearing the end of my routine, I ignore the increased throbbing pain as I perform three grand jetés. It is only on the third jeté, when my toes reach the floor, that I feel as if I've just landed on a bed of hot coals. As my body collapses, all I can think is that I will never get into Performing Arts now. It's over.

I lift my head from the floor and stare at the dance masters, and they're all smiling, calling out “Bravo!” From the reaction of everyone else around me, I realize that I must have done well despite my disastrous ending. Before I know it, Spencer and one of the other students carry me downstairs to the school infirmary.

Daddy is beside my bed holding my hand. The nurse explains to us that, because of the pain I'm in, it would be best if she cut the shoes off my feet. Daddy and I watch as she carefully cuts the shoes from the heel to the middle of my foot, instantly, the leather falls away. Taking extra care with the toes, the top of the shoe slips off. My toes are practically raw. Daddy holds my hand tight.

After several warm towels and a pound of ointment, the nurse gently bandages each toe. I have to laugh because my feet look like they are wearing miniature white hats. I'm told to rest a while and then we can go home. She hands Daddy a pair of crutches and says she will be back soon with written instructions for Daddy on how to take care of the inflamed toes when we get home. She takes my shoes and puts them in a plastic bag.

"Don't you worry now, do as I tell you, and you will be fine in a week or so."

Her warm and sympathetic smile makes me relax for the first time today. "By the way, I probably shouldn't be telling you this, but I think you deserve to hear something nice." She looks around to make sure no one else is around. "Everyone is talking about your audition and your courageous effort. The word is that you were amazing and a true professional."

Daddy gazes at me with pride. So today wasn't such a disaster after all. I did dazzle them.

Daddy has brushed my hair, and packed my dance bag, and we are waiting for the nurse to come back. When she walks into the room, she looks disturbed. "Mr. Rosen, I think you need to see this."

The nurse hands my father my ballet shoes. The lining has been torn. "There was something not right about these shoes. I took the liberty to do this, and, well, here is what I found." She opens up the palm of her hand and shows us what amounts to two thimbles of salt crystals.

"Now I don't know how this got into the lining of these shoes, but I would call that store and get my money back. Why, you might even think about suing them!"

Trying to control his anger, Daddy takes the shoes and stuffs them into his jacket pocket. He says in a low voice but clear enough for me to hear, "You will be punished."

Sarah

Audition Day

I am good, I am kind, I am smart, I am beautiful, I will no longer doubt myself AND I will be accepted by Performing Arts because I will knock them dead! Ok, here goes!

I enter Studio 406, cool and calm. There are four drama teachers - three women, and one man - seated at a long table. The women don't look anything like my teachers at school; they are sophisticated movie-types. One of them has a pair of cats-eye shaped glasses with rhinestones. I could kill for those, I love them so much. The other woman is wearing all black, and her hair is done up in a large bun with cherry red chopsticks holding it together. Her lipstick matches. The third is an older woman with silver hair cut short enough to pass for a man's cut. Her lips are painted in bright orange. All three are fabulous. The man is another story. He has the shiniest bald head I've ever seen. He reminds me of Mr. Miller, the pickle man at our neighborhood deli. This makes me relax right away and I have to hold back from giggling. He's the first one to speak. He introduces himself as Mr. Ordway, head of the Drama Department, and then he introduces the other three drama teachers. I smile and wait for them to tell me to start.

"Well, Miss Lanin, why do you want to be an actress?"

Miss Prescott told me that they might surprise me with a question I was not prepared for. But the answer to this one I know by heart. I instantly imagine myself lifting a veil off my face and automatically transforming into the actress I am meant to be. Hopefully, these four people in front of me will see that, too.

After my interview and improvisational exercise, I begin my two monologues. Each one lasts two minutes. I perform with complete confidence and ease. When I finish the audition, I look them in their eyes and say thank you and goodbye. Walking down the stairway, I stare with envy at the students who pass by me. I wish so much to be part of them, part of this school.

I push open the large wooden doors to the street and walk down the steps as gracefully and nonchalantly as I can. Mom, looking nervous, is pacing back and forth on the sidewalk, just where I left her this morning.

"Mom, I did it!" I shout out with happiness.

All at once we're jumping into each other's arms. After a lot of hugging and tears of relief and joy, we link our arms together and walk down to Horn & Hardart on Broadway. Over lunch, I tell her everything about the audition.

"I feel I've got a really good shot at getting in. Everything was perfect. Thanks for your support, Mom, and I'll also have to thank Michael. I wouldn't have gone ahead with this if it hadn't been for the two of you. And, if for some reason I don't get in, then it will be both of your faults." We break out laughing and don't stop till we get home.

As soon as I'm in my room; I sit down and compose a letter to Michael.

Dear Michael, I'm so grateful to you for making me believe in myself, working with me almost every night the last few weeks, giving me the journal. You were right, as always, how writing your feelings down can release a lot of anger. It has and, to prove it, hard as it may be to believe, I even called Lila last night and wished her luck tomorrow on her audition. She was speechless and, after a second or two, she hung up. That was OK; I wasn't upset. I would probably have reacted the same way if she had called me. And, by the way, I know that you will do great in your interview next week because it's you who is the truly gifted one. Love you, Michael. You are the best friend ever.

I read the letter to make sure it is right, fold it, put it into an envelope, and seal it with a kiss. I call Michael and ask him if he wants to meet me at Tar Beach.

The air is so fresh and the sun is warm enough for us to feel comfortable in my beach chairs. We settle in as if we are a married couple. I had brought up two Cokes and a bag of chips. We make a toast to our future and I give Michael my letter. When he finishes, he takes my hand and says that it should be him thanking me. Michael sits back and gives me one of his most wonderful smiles and says he's ready to hear everything.

I give him a blow by blow of the audition. By the time I'm finished, I'm actually exhausted. I don't think I took a breath once. Then Michael hits me with a surprise question. "Did you hear anything about how Lila did today?"

I was so wrapped up in myself that I had not thought about her at all.

"No, I haven't, but I wouldn't be surprised if, by the time we go downstairs, Lila will already be sitting in my kitchen bragging to Mom about how fabulous she was."

Since I don't want to spoil my perfect day, I turn the conversation to him and ask about his upcoming audition. I listen to some of his doubts and boost his confidence as he had done for me, and I tell him that he will definitely be accepted into Music and Art. We talk for a while longer and Michael says he should be getting home. Before we go down, I ask him if he's changed his mind at all about when to tell his father, since the audition is only a week away. He hesitates, puts his hands in his pockets, and walks over to the edge of the roof. Suddenly it's like he's gone off into a private place in his head. I give him space and wait. After a few seconds he turns around and goes about putting the beach chairs away, and we both clean up the remains of our celebration. Michael's silence is enough for me to know that he doesn't want to talk about his father. I follow him downstairs.

When we enter my apartment, the first thing we hear is the voice of Minnie, talking a mile a minute and Selma repeating every word her sister is saying, "and there's Max carrying Lila in his arms, up the stairs, just like she's a wounded bird." "So pale she looked," says Minnie with wide-eyed wonder. "So very pale. Terrible. Poor girl, and those toes all bandaged up, just terrible."

"Poor girl," says Selma, talking over Minnie.

"But the best part is that he brought her home by TAXI! Can you imagine how much that must have cost, Hannah?" Minnie asks.

"A fortune that cost, that's what," says Selma. "Hmm. Wonder what Max is doing to make all that money? Taxis, all those lessons and more lessons. He caters to that girl, nothing too good for his angel. And poor Fritzy gets nothing. No wonder she's . . ."

"Enough!" shouts out Mom." I think it is time to go, and, ladies, I think you should stop worrying about how Max makes his money. That is his business, and no more talk about Fritzy. Right now, we should be good neighbors and see if there is anything we can do for Lila."

Minnie and Selma aren't happy about being dismissed by Mom. They both leave in a huff. Mom immediately gives me the same look that she gave the sisters, making it very clear that what she said to the two of them goes for me, too.

"I am going over there now. Sarah, do you want to come with me?"

Normally I would say no, but I'm curious as hell about those toes. I'm about to ask Michael if he wants to come with us, but Mom leads Michael to the door. "I think for now it should just be me and Sarah. She will call you tonight."

A few seconds later we're standing outside the Rosens' apartment. Mom rings the doorbell. We wait, but no one comes. Mom then rings the bell again and follows with two loud knocks on the door. We hear the sound of shuffling footsteps approaching. Fritzy opens up the door with the safety chain on. Since I'm standing directly in back of Mom, I can't see anything, but Mom sees enough to make her gasp. Without turning around, and in a low but stern voice, she says, "Go home now, Sarah."

I walk away and hear the Rosens' door closing after Mom.

Lila

Lila Comes Home

As soon as we step out of the taxi, I look up and she's there at the window, staring at us. I bet she's been there all day, waiting . . . waiting. I don't know what she expected, but it wasn't this. The sympathy from our neighbors, Daddy's face stretched so tight with anger as he carries me in his arms, my bandaged toes, my pain . . . have drained all the color from her face. How stupid she is!

When Daddy and I get out of the elevator, the door to the apartment is already open. Mom steps back into the living room. She tries to look believably upset at the sight of my toes stiffly pointing upwards, the telltale evidence of her calculating plan. Anger starts to bubble up in me, but, when I lock my eyes into hers, all I want to do is cry out *why do you hate me so much, why?* She comes towards us, but Daddy pushes her out of the way with his shoulder and we go into my bedroom. With his foot, he kicks the door closed, loud enough for the whole building to hear.

Daddy lays me down on my bed, props up my pillows, and takes extra care putting a blanket over me to make sure that my toes aren't covered and so there is no pressure on them. He tells me to try and rest. He has to go out to the drugstore to get more bandages and ointment.

"Daddy, please don't leave me alone with her, please!"

"Lila, she won't hurt you anymore . . . I promise."

Daddy closes the door and leaves me. I want to get up and lock it but the pain is too bad. I can't stand up on my own. I'd give anything to close my eyes and go to sleep, but I can hear her heavy breathing on the other side of my door, which means I can't trust her. I know she is capable of anything.

Sarah

Sarah Waits Up For Hannah

I've been going over all the things that happened today - the audition, how good I felt about it, how proud Mom was of me, and how Michael beamed with pride. That meant the most to me because there was no way I would have made it without him. Then, of course, the extra bonus of my most glorious day was listening to Minnie and Selma, the two best gossips in the South Bronx, tell all about Lila's surprising homecoming. It could not have been a more delicious ending because this meant that she may possibly have failed her auditions, which one I didn't know and didn't care! But then something strange happened to me. As the two sisters continued to speak, I imagined Lila being carried up, in pain, and scared, and I was suddenly having mixed feelings. One part of me was wickedly taking it all in, and the other part of me was filled with sympathy.

I wonder how badly she's hurt. Did she even finish her auditions? I understand how important this day was for her, for all of us - but maybe more so for Lila. She and Max have been working for this a long time - forever really.

Meanwhile, it's almost midnight and Mom is still at the Rosens' apartment. What's going on over there? I leave my bedroom and walk into the living room where Daddy is watching TV.

"Daddy, don't you think you should go over and see what's keeping Mom?"

"Baby, I've been married to your mother for a long time - if she wants me to be there, she would have let me know already. I only jump when she tells me."

"But, Dad," I say in a whining voice.

"No buts. Go to bed. I'm sure there'll be plenty to hear in the morning."

Still frustrated, I mumble some not so nice words under my breath and go back to my room. It's not likely that I'm going to fall asleep because, besides my triumph, my mind keeps going back to when Fritzy carefully opened the door, only as wide as the safety chain allowed, preventing us from seeing her whole face but not her swollen black and blue eye.

I have no idea what time Mom came home last night. Because I wanted to make sure I got to talk to her this morning before going to school, I set my clock a half hour early. When I walk into the kitchen, Mom and Dad are sitting at the kitchen table, heads close together and whispering in Yiddish. This is what they do when they don't want me to know certain things. Not a good sign. I drop my backpack on the floor to let them know I'm here, and they automatically stop speaking.

"How is Lila?"

Mom gets up from the table right away, goes to the stove, and starts breaking some eggs into a frying pan. As she is doing this, her back is to me. Another bad sign. She doesn't want me to see that she is worried.

"She should be fine in a week or two," Mom says.

"That's good. So what happened?"

Mom turns around slowly and stares at me. It's easy to see that she's worried and I can tell by the seriousness of her expression that she's not sure of how much to tell me. She goes back to finishing my eggs and serves them to me. "It was an accident. Sarah, if anyone asks, that's what you tell them. Understand?"

Without saying goodbye, she walks out of the kitchen. I hear the door to her bedroom close.

"Dad, what's going on?"

He gets up from the chair, picks up my backpack and hands it to me, ushering me to the door. "Your Momma has had a long night. Go to school now, enjoy your day, and, Sarah, remember what she said. It was an accident, that's all it was."

"Right, will do."

When I get downstairs, Michael is already outside waiting for me. Looking anxious and impatient, he takes me by the arm and we start walking. At the corner, he pulls me over to the side of a building." So where did she go? What did your mother tell you?"

"Nothing, she told me nothing. Where did who go," I ask.

"Fritzy! While your mother was at the Rosens', Max left with Fritzy and came back without her."

"How the hell do you know that?"

"Your mother called mine and told her. Max took Fritzy away?"

Lila

Later That Night

She's back, her smell so overpowering that it fills my lungs. Oh, my God, she's on top of me. Her weight is crushing me deep down into my mattress. I can't breathe, I'm suffocating! I scream for her to get off me. I beg her, please, but she just laughs and laughs and then the mattress swallows me up! "Lila, wake up sweetheart, it's OK! You are having a bad dream. I am here, everything is all right!" Daddy's arms are wrapped so tightly around me that it's still hard to breathe. My whole body is shaking, and my toes feel ten times their normal size. They are bursting to get free from the bandages; the bandages are strangling them. The pain is unbearable.

"Why does she hate me so much? Why Daddy?"

Daddy lets go of me and gently lays me back down on my bed. I swallow the pill that he gives me and I hold onto his hand. I'm so scared of going back to sleep. I ask him not to leave me. Daddy says something to me but his voice sounds far away. His hand slips out of mine and I feel like I'm falling, falling.

Someone is caressing my hair and humming a tune so sweet it almost sounds like a lullaby. I open my eyes thinking that it's Daddy but, to my surprise, it's Hannah. I look around to see if I'm really awake, if I am in my room. If she's here, something must have happened to Daddy. A sudden panic sweeps over me.

"Where's Daddy, Hannah? Where is he?"

"He is fine, Lila. He had to go to work. There is nothing for you to be worried about."

But she's wrong, because, in my last dream, Daddy hurt Mom badly and he was taken away. What wasn't a dream was the look Daddy had in his eyes when the nurse showed him my shoes. That terrified me.

As much as I hate Mom, I don't want Daddy to get into trouble because, then, what would happen to me?

Michael

Audition Day

I was told that I would not have the opportunity to discuss my portfolio. The process was that artwork would be returned after the drawing exams and then applicants would be notified in a few weeks whether or not they had been accepted to Music and Art.

When the exams are finished, Mr. Laurence, head of the Art Department, thanks all of us and tells us we are free to go. As I pick up my portfolio and prepare to leave the studio, he asks me to please stay behind. The other students all shoot me a look that ranges from interest to suspicion. Immediately I get the gut feeling that he is going to say that today was a waste of time and there is no way that I will be going to Music and Art. At the same time, the image of Father's face looms over me, raging at what I have done.

"Mr. Stein, are you all right? You look a bit pale," Mr. Laurence asks.

"No, sir, I'm fine. I guess I'm just a little nervous."

"No need to be. Please sit down. I would like to take a little more time to look over your work."

Mr. Laurence looks through my artwork slowly. When he gets to the graphite portraits, he stops. He carefully studies each of them. It's hard to tell what he's thinking because his face remains expressionless.

"Mmm, interesting, very," Mr. Laurence says.

Slowly, he picks his head up, cups his chin and stares at me. I think he's about to ask me a question but only stares at me, and then he bends his head forward, close enough to the portraits that his face is almost right on top of the paper. I have a vision that Mr. Laurence's small wisps of hair are going to transform into droplets of water that fall on each of the portraits and make them disappear. I'm wondering if I made the right decision choosing the ones that I did. At first, I had decided that I wouldn't include the ones of Tommy; they were too personal. But, when I put them together with the ones of Mother, Sarah, and the Maestro, they somehow worked.

"These are good. Exceptional, even," says Mr. Laurence.

"Thank you," I answer as humbly as possible.

"Your bio states that you have been studying the violin for years and only started drawing for the last two years. Is that true?"

"Yes, sir. Before that, I doodled, did some sketches, played with charcoal, colored pencils, that kind of thing. But two years is about right," I answer.

"Well, looking at your work, I doubt that anything you have drawn would be considered doodling. Now, I should not be telling you this, but I believe you . . . have the makings of a truly gifted artist," Mr. Laurence says, looking at me earnestly.

With that, he closes the portfolio and places it in my art bag along with my other work. Mr. Laurence gets up from his chair, and shakes my hand, and bids me good-bye.

Once I'm in the street, I want to shout out for everyone to hear. I am Michael Stein and I am going to be an artist, live in Paris, and become famous! I can't wait to tell Mother and Sarah and Father. I'm praying that once he hears what the head of the Art Department told me, he'll be fine, maybe even proud. I can only hope.

A few steps away from the entrance to the train station is a phone booth. Excited, I step in, take some dimes from my pocket, drop one in and call Mother. No answer. I hang up and try Sarah. If she's not there, at least Hannah will be. But again no luck; no one picks up. Disappointed, I head downstairs into the subway.

Seated on the train, I look around to see if there is a kind face, just one person with whom I can share my news, but all the passengers have their heads buried in their newspapers, are sleeping, or are just staring into space. By the third stop, I'm ready to explode! The train comes to a jerky halt and the doors open. Bainbridge Avenue is the station. Tommy's father's bakery is one block away. I jump out of my seat and run out the doors. My watch says four o'clock. I know Tommy has got to be there by now, and I have to tell someone before I burst.

Mr. DeMarco and Tommy are filled with congratulations and praise. Mr. DeMarco shouts out to all his customers, boastful as if I were his son. Soon the customers are all kissing me and slapping me on the back. Meanwhile, Tommy is standing to the side, watching it all and smiling at me. When I leave the bakery, I am loaded with two shopping bags of cakes and cookies. I am feeling so loved that I don't want to leave, but I have one more stop to make before I go home. When I leave the Maestro and the Signora an hour and a half later, I get another bag of cookies and tons of kisses.

Riding high from the audition and the joyous time spent with everyone, I run into the apartment and shout out for Mother. Something stops me. In the middle of the living room floor are my sketchbooks, and sheets of drawings along with boxes of colored pencils all carefully arranged in a perfect circle. I slowly lift my head up. Chills travel down my spine.

Pointing right at me are Father's highly polished black shoes, tapping away creepily. Tap. Tap. Tap. Standing up as tall as I can, I look straight at him. On his lap are my portraits of Tommy, including nude ones. I have no choice now but to face the inevitable and pray that the cement-like lump in my throat will not suffocate me.

Father gets up, deliberately letting everything slide off his lap onto the floor. Coming towards me, he steps on the drawings and with one foot forcefully sweeps the rest of the pads and pencils out of his way. I watch as my work flies across the room.

"And what is this filth?"

Before I can answer or defend myself in any way, his hand

smacks me across the face. The sheer strength of his anger forces me to my knees. My hands fold over my head as he comes down on me with his fists. When I think it's over, he delivers one more blow and breaks my arm, then I feel the stabbing pain of a cracked rib. Suddenly, there is the piercing sound of someone screaming. Only then does he stop.

Lila

One Week Later

Daddy has taken the week off. He stays with me all day, except for when he goes to get groceries. Then Hannah comes in to keep me company. When he comes back, there is always a special treat. Flowers, chocolates, and, once, cannolis from Tommy's father's bakery. Daddy doesn't like Tommy. He warns me to stay away from him.

"Boys like that are trouble."

The other day Daddy brought home a Polaroid camera. He takes pictures of me all day, posing in hundreds of positions. Some of them are beautiful and some are just plain hilarious.

Hannah brought Sarah with her yesterday, and she was being so nice. I believe she really feels bad for me. We took pictures of the three of us and a few of just Sarah and me. Later that night I stared at them, and I swear we looked like we have always been best friends. It was strange, but it made me feel good. I put the photos under my pillow.

Since Mom tried to sabotage me, there have been surprising changes. For the first time, I'm not anxious, angry, or scared. Of course, a lot has to do with the fact that Daddy took Mom to his cousin's place in Queens.

Mom calls at night when she thinks I'm in bed. Daddy

doesn't say a lot. Mostly he listens and hangs up. He never tells me what they talk about, and, truthfully I don't care. I hope she never comes back and everything stays as it is.

Sarah

Sitting With Michael And Lila

Roxy says I've taken on the role of visiting nurse. Since Lila's and Michael's "accidents", my afternoons and evenings are filled with spending time with the two of them.

Michael gets the afternoons after school. We've developed a routine. By the time I get there, Mrs. Stein has cocoa and cookies waiting. I bring them to Michael. He usually watches me eat with gusto and listens to my gossip of the day. I tell him silly stuff and leave out that the whole school is buzzing about what happened, let alone the endless questions. I'm asked, day in and day out: Is his arm ever going to be right again? When's he coming back to school? Where's his dad? And the rumors, oh, my God! Some of the people on the block are wondering how come Dudley was with Mrs. Stein. Is there, heaven forbid, something going on between them? Funny, that's all they can concentrate on. They also seem to have forgotten that Mom was there, too. But the most bizarre rumor is since Fritzy and Mr. Stein are missing in action, whether they have run away with each other. When I heard that I couldn't stop laughing, and then, for one minute, I thought to myself, *What if?* They're both evil enough. Anyway, Michael doesn't need to hear all that and, truthfully, he never asks. Actually, we hardly talk about what happened at all. As close as we are, he still keeps secrets from me and I've come to accept that.

For the rest of the afternoon until I leave we sit close together on his bed and read to each other a chapter from each of our books. Mine right now is *Breakfast at Tiffany's* and I'm loving it to pieces. I want to grow up and be just like the main character Holly Golightly. Michael's book is *A Movable Feast* by Ernest Hemmingway, a memoir about Hemingway's time in Paris in the nineteen twenties and the famous artists and writers who lived there. After we finish, we talk about our dreams. They never change. Michael's is to be a famous artist and live in Paris, and mine is to be a famous actress of stage and screen and, eventually, we will live together in Paris forever and ever! But I never tell him the last part.

After two hours, our time comes to an end. I'm so relaxed and happy that I don't mind that, when I get home, Lila will be there. Mom brings her to our apartment in the morning, and she stays till Max comes home from work. Once her bandages come off, which is next week, she'll be going back to school.

No matter how odd this sounds, I have to say that having her around hasn't been all that bad. Lila's become quiet. Most of the time, she's lost in her own head. I can't blame her. But still, even though I do feel sorry for her, I still can't totally trust her. Well, at least Fritzy is gone, which is a good thing, but for how long?

Tonight after supper we're in my room and I can see she's got something on her mind, so I ask her if she's OK. "I think so, but I'd like to tell you what happened at the dance audition."

Lila puts down her crutches and sits beside me on the bed so that her face is looking forward and not at me. Lila speaks in a mellow tone, not her usual Drama Queen bit, and tells me about the dance audition. When she says that at the end of the audition she wanted to die, I believe her.

But what's really getting to me is that I'm taking no joy in her humiliation and injury. Maybe all the events of the last few weeks have affected me, too. This is what Mom must mean when she says, "Sometimes you have to let go." Lila turns to look at me and stares right into my eyes and says, "I realize that acting is not for me; it never was. I don't have it, but you do. You're meant to be an actress."

My head is spinning. Not in a million years would I ever think that Lila Rosen would say she wasn't perfect at something and that I was! Before I have a chance to take this all in, the bedroom door opens; Max and Mom enter the bedroom, each holding up an envelope. Max says, "Well here it is. Who wants to open hers first?"

Lila

I Can Never Believe Him Again

I can't believe what he's saying. I won't listen. I can't! It's horrible. Instead, I'll think of only good things, like the time that I spend with Hannah each day till Daddy comes home. How Sarah and I sit and talk, and play cards or games while Hannah is making dinner. How Leo makes me laugh by telling awful jokes. How Sarah made a toast to our acceptance into Performing Arts. At first, when I asked her if she was OK with it, she looked unsure, like her worst nightmare was going to happen, but then she jumped off the couch, ran into the kitchen, and came back with two Cokes. She raised her bottle in the air and announced that she was making a toast to us. That we are becoming friends is stupendous, but the best part is that, when Daddy comes to take me home, it's only the two of us. Then one night he gives me the news. When he puts his arms around me and tries to hold me, I pull away from him in disgust.

"I have to allow her back. I swear to you, Lila, it will be different . . . It won't be forever. You have to trust me. It's just that I can't keep having Hannah take care of you; she has her own family to take care of."

As tears roll down his face, he's pleading with me to

believe him. I put my hands to my ears and shut his voice out. I can never believe him again. The only thing I know for sure now is that one day I will leave with or . . . without him.

Michael

Two Weeks Later

The cast comes off my arm in two weeks and my broken rib is healing. I think about his attack. Sarah told me that her dad and Mr. Dudley managed to get in a few punches at Father before the police came.

I didn't know until after I woke up in the hospital that the police had put Father in jail. I took pleasure in imagining the humiliation he must have felt as the neighbors, people he normally looked down on as inferior, all watched him being taken away in handcuffs.

To my surprise, he was released a few days later when Mom dropped the charges. I have no idea where he is; Mother won't tell me. I don't really care - I just don't want him to come back. What bothers me is that I sense that Mother worries about him. Truthfully, it hurts me to see that she still cares about him. I don't understand how that's possible after all he's done to both of us.

Sarah and Tommy both have asked me a few times how I feel about the whole thing. When I say nothing, they look at me as if I am just trying to cover up my feelings. I'm not. If I have any, they're somewhere deep inside me. And that's where I want them to stay.

As close as I feel to the two of them, I can't ever see them or anyone understanding what it was like to grow up with someone like Father, to understand what his acts of violence have done to me. Yet the other day I realized there is someone - Lila.

April

Lila

Daddy's Surprise

It's beginning to get dark. Daddy packs his camera away. He's been taking pictures of me for the last two hours. Usually, I have fun when he does this, but not so much anymore. But just like a model, I still smile, pose, and do whatever he asks me too.

"Lila, honey, are you OK? You didn't enjoy today did you?"

"I'm fine, just tired," I say, not caring whether he believes me or not.

We walk to our favorite spot, a bench that is underneath a huge maple tree and sit down. Daddy likes it here because it's quiet and hidden away. He puts his hand in his pocket and gives me a small gold box. "It's a surprise. I was going to give it to you next week for your birthday, but you look so low today . . . this should cheer you up."

I open the box. Inside are two tickets for *Bye Bye Birdie* on Broadway.

"I know it can't make up for everything that has happened, but I promise that this birthday will be the best you have ever had. Oh, and it's opening night!" he says with excitement.

At any other time, I would be bowled over, giving him a thousand kisses. He tells me that we're also going to Sardi's before the show. He's convinced that someone famous will see me and I will be discovered.

My lips brush his cheek. I sit back and give him a forced smile. "Thank you, Daddy, I know it will be a wonderful evening." My words sound empty and he knows it. I've hurt his feelings.

"Lila, listen, I know it's hard having Mom back. But she's there only to clean, make meals, and take care of our needs; that's all. I have given her rules and she has no choice but to obey them. She needs us because she has nowhere to go, and we need her for a time until we are ready."

Until we are ready; that's a laugh! Up until the night Daddy told me that Mom was coming home, I was happy.

Her being gone was the best thing that ever happened. The kindness that Hannah, Leo, and neighbors have given me has made me feel I matter. Sarah sitting with me each afternoon and evening, talking and laughing just like girlfriends was the icing on the cake. Each day the boogeyman in my head was slipping away. And best of all is that, even though Mom's act of sabotage failed, she still lost and I won. I got into Performing Arts. That fact gives me great satisfaction. The only thing that would be better is that her disgrace festers into a boil and she rots!

Now I have to tell Sarah that I won't be coming to our birthday party because of Daddy's gift. For sure, she's going to be disappointed, then curious, then just plain angry that she didn't get invited, too. And I don't blame her. If it was Hannah who got the tickets, Sarah would automatically say that I had to come, too. But I can't do that. When Daddy and I are alone, we're not like other fathers and daughters, we're different. Her being with us would change the evening - he would be too jealous. No, she can't go with us. I'm embarrassed to see her, so I'm just going to write a note and slip it under her door. Our friendship was too good to be true anyway. After she reads my note, we'll probably end up just returning to our old ways.

And this will be Daddy's fault. He's lied to me again; he's weak. There will never just be the two of us far, far away, never. It's all too clear to me now. Who knows, maybe Mom did win.

Sarah

But It's Our Birthday!

Mom hands me a lilac-colored envelope. I know right away who it's from. I tear it open. I can't believe what I'm reading:

"Dear Sarah, I know you're going to be angry but I can't come to our birthday party, Daddy is taking me to Sardi's for dinner and to the opening of Bye Bye Birdie on Broadway. I can't believe it's happening. Can you imagine, opening night? I am so thrilled and excited. Sorry."

Yeah, right! I can only imagine. After all that Mom did for Max and Lila, and how I went out of my way to be nice to her, you'd think he would have gotten another ticket for me. Mom says it had to have cost a fortune, and two tickets were way more than he probably could afford, let alone a third ticket. Ok, I get that, but Lila could have at least said how she wished I was going with her. That might have made me feel just a teensy bit better. But no, instead she leaves a note under the door . . . really! Well, I don't give a damn; the party will be great without her.

Mom sees me sulking and sits down next to me. "I know you're upset, but Lila has been through so much the last few weeks and, now with Fritzy back, it can't be good. I am glad Max can do it for her. She deserves it."

Since Fritzy has come back, I've hardly seen Lila at all, and when I do, she seems to be avoiding me. Maybe it's because she knew of the tickets way before, or it's about Fritzy. I don't know. As far as Fritzy goes, no one sees her except when she goes out grocery shopping. She doesn't talk to anyone, and most people keep their heads down when she passes them by. She doesn't even sit at her window looking out on the street like she always did.

Mom and Dad were talking about it the other night. As usual, Dad thinks that things are not kosher with the Rosens. "You know Hannah, this *meshugaas* between Max and Fritzy goes back to the DP camp. He never should have married her. She lied to him for sure."

Mom puts her hand over his mouth. "Leo, keep quiet. No more, you hear me? No more talk about this!"

Of course, he had more he wanted to say ... and I wanted to hear it, but Mom told me to go to my room. I did, but I kept my door open enough to hear her read him the Riot Act.

"Sarah does not need to hear all that business. It was a long time ago, and Fritzy has paid for it because Max doesn't let her forget. Anyway, it's their business, not ours. So stop talking about it and keep your suspicions to yourself."

"All right, but what about the money? Where's he getting all that dough? Can you tell me that?"

The next thing I hear is Mom walking out the door. When she's down or upset, she takes a walk. Tonight I think it is going to be a long one. Meanwhile, I'm no longer thinking about *Bye Bye Birdie*. I'm too curious about what happened between Fritzy and Max way back when.

Michael

The Birthday Party

When I get to the party, the first thing I notice is that Lila isn't there. Sarah is in a huddle talking to some of the girls, so I asked Mrs. Lanin. When she tells me what happened, I am really surprised why Sarah didn't tell me. It's not like her to keep anything from me, especially when it has to do with Lila. Sarah sees me, leaves the girls, and comes to me. She whispers in my ear.

"If you ask me anything about you know who, I will freak out! Now come and dance with me; it's my birthday and we're going to have a blast!"

And we do. Mrs. Lanin goes all out. She and Mr. Lanin bring out two cakes. One is Sarah's birthday cake, and the other has both our names on it, with our new schools, Performing Arts and Music and Art, underneath them. Lila's name is missing from both. Mr. Lanin proceeds to give a loving and cheery speech about how special we were and sings out more than a dozen *mazel tovs*. I am very happy. When I get home, I fall straight into bed. No bad dreams tonight.

The phone wakes me up from a deep sleep. I look at my clock. It's only five-thirty in the morning. I look outside my window. It's still dark. My clock says five-thirty a.m. Who can be calling at this hour? What if it's Father? Should I answer it before Mom? Is he calling to ask to come back? I jump out of bed and run into the kitchen, hoping I get to it before Mom. The ringing stops. I start to feel panicky. *Please God, don't let it be him. He can't come back, he can't!*

Daylight slowly streams into the kitchen. The phone rings again. I make a dive for it.

"Was it nice?" Lila asks in a ghostly voice.

I answer "Yes." I ask about her evening on the town. There is a long pause. The phone goes dead. I think about calling her back, but I know she won't pick up. Did something happen last night? Did her Mother hurt her? Where is her Father? Crazy thoughts start running through my head.

Lila's having to face her mother every day after what she did to her has to be unbearable. God knows I wouldn't be able to do it. If Father came back, I would only want to hurt him as bad as he did me . . . or even worse. Maybe I should just let worrying about Lila go and not start any trouble. I'll wait till Mother wakes up. She and Mrs. Lanin will know what to do.

Part Three

1960

May – August

May

Lila

Fritzy Breaks Down

Except for a few words, I haven't heard Mom speak since she's been back. She's obeyed Daddy's rules of silence. She behaves like a servant instead of a Mom and wife. The sound of her sorrowful voice wakes me up. Her words are mumbled and I can't make out what she's saying. Today is Saturday and all I want is to hide under my covers till Daddy comes back. He's got another weekend of overtime, but tonight he'll be home a little earlier and has promised to take me to China Moon for dinner. So, if he's working, who is she talking to, herself or someone else?

I open my door and am shocked by what I see. Mom is on her knees, her arms wrapped around Daddy's legs. He tries to pull away as she holds on to him for dear life. I look up at Daddy. The disgust on his face makes me cringe.

"Max, please let me come with you. I can't live like this . . . the loneliness is killing me . . . I've done everything you have asked of me. "Please," begs Mom.

Dad bends down and pushes her away. She falls back against the couch. Sitting there with her legs apart, she looks like a deflated, blown up, life-size doll. Daddy commands her to get up. Her face hardens. With the back of her hands, she wipes her tears away and yells, "It was because of me, a *goy* peasant that you did not get caught by the Germans and die in the camps along with all the other Jews. I hid you. Don't ever forget that it is from here." Mom pulls her dress up and grabs her vagina. "It is from here that your spoiled whore of a daughter came from."

Daddy takes a fist and punches her in the eye. "And I will never understand how so beautiful a child could come out of someone so ugly and rotten." Daddy raises his hand once again.

I can't watch anymore. I shout at him to stop.

"No, Daddy, don't!"

The two of them are so surprised by my voice that they stare at me as if they don't know me. All at once I'm overcome . . . drowning in waves of guilt, disgust, and pity.

"How long have you been listening?" Daddy asks.

I ignore his question. I wish I had never seen or heard the horrible words that came out of Mom's mouth. But what was worse was watching Daddy striking out at her the way he did. I'm shaking so badly I can hardly stand. All I can think about is if I hadn't walked in, God knows how far he would have gone. Daddy reaches towards me. I'm afraid for him to touch me. For the first time, I wonder if he could ever hurt me.

"Lila, go get dressed. We are leaving." I do as he says.

Fifteen minutes later, we are at the park, We sit under our special tree. A large maple that hides us from everyone else. My strength caves, and fear gets the better of me. Daddy leans his head towards mine, and I become lost in memories of being a little girl. When I cried, he would name each tear, his soft breath blowing them into the air. Suddenly, Daddy's lips touch mine - his mouth tastes sour. His kisses become rough, desperate. I feel helpless. My thoughts are running wild in my head. I'm torn between guilt and excitement. I throw my arms around his neck. I know that what we are doing is wrong.

I want to stop so we can talk. I'm about to loosen my hold on him when he pushes me away and jumps up from the bench. He turns every which way to see if someone is out there.

"Oh, my God, is someone watching us?" I ask.

"It's only the wind," he says. "But we should go."

I pray he's right.

Sarah

At The Park With Michael

Mom is out tonight with Mrs. Stein. Dad has a card game. I'm supposed to stay home and study for a big history test on Friday, but I've been at it for an hour and I'm feeling antsy. I go to the fridge, where Mom's left some roast beef for dinner, but I really would like a pizza and some company. I call Michael.

"How about a pizza?"

"Can't; have a test. Don't you have one too?" Michael asks.

"Yes, but I'm finished and you don't need to study because you're brilliant. Besides, it's a beautiful spring evening and school's practically over anyway."

In ten minutes we are on our way. As usual, we talk about our new schools in the fall, and I also bring up summer jobs. "We should try to get jobs at the concession stands at Orchard Beach for the summer." I ask him if he's still interested and, to my great surprise, he says he already has a job working for Tommy's father at the bakery, making deliveries.

"Wow, when did that happen?" I ask.

"A few weeks ago. I meant to tell you but just had other things on my mind."

I know that Michael and Tommy have become friends, and

he's crazy about Mr. DeMarco. I'm feeling a bit jealous.

"Hey, you Ok?" he asks.

"Sure, good for you. Better bring home some of those goodies," I say, trying to make light of it but not really feeling that way at all.

I know I'm being silly, but I'm disappointed that he didn't tell me about the job. Michael can tell I'm not happy. "Come on, Sarah, let's go to the park; the ice cream truck should still be there. My treat. Then we can go to the fountain, put our feet in the water, and talk about Paris."

OK, he's won me over. I can't resist ice cream, and I love talking about our dreams of being famous and living in Paris. Besides, it's hard to stay mad at Michael, if not impossible.

We finish our ice cream, and I get a sudden urge to pee. The bathrooms are on the other side of the park, and I'm not allowed to go in there. All sorts of nasty things happen there, so I really don't have a choice other than going into the bushes.

"Michael, I've got to seriously tinkle!" I say as I scout out where to go. "Over there, come on, quick; you stand guard."

Michael takes his position and I make my way into a hedge of bushes. As soon as I pull my pants down, I hear weird sounds. Probably some older kids making out somewhere. Under the trees is a popular spot. Hope to hell they can't see me. I curse under my breath and pull my pants up. I'm not sure if I can hold it in, but, until I know what's going on, I'll have to. I get on my knees and peep through the thick leaves. Even though it's almost dark, the lamppost behind me gives out enough light to make out a couple sitting on a bench only a few feet away. I think the woman is crying. The man, trying to calm her, gives her little pecks on her cheeks, her eyes, and forehead; he ever so softly combs her hair with his hand. He takes her face in his hands. Hypnotized by what I'm seeing, I don't realize that the gentleness of the moment is now changing into something that's anything but.

The man is now pressing his mouth down on her hard enough that she seems to be struggling to breathe. For a second I think she wants to pull away, but instead, she puts her arms around his neck and they are both locked into their passion. Confused at how the moment has changed, I lose my balance, stumble backwards against the bushes. A rustling sound ricochets. I put my hand over my mouth and curl up as small as possible. I pray that Michael doesn't say my name. Nervously, the man jumps up from the bench, nervously looking in every direction. Still suspicious, he takes hold of the woman and they scurry out of the park. They pass right by me, I become frozen. It's Lila and Max.

I'm so shocked that I'm not aware of Michael asking me, "Sarah, what's going on? How long does it take?"

"Michael, did you see anyone go by just now?"

"I did, looked like they were in a hurry, why?"

Something stops me from spilling it all out. Who will believe me anyway? It's just too gross.

When I get home, Mom and Dad are in the kitchen. I yell "I love you. I'm tired. " When Mom comes in later to say goodnight. I pretend to be asleep. I know for sure that sleep will not come easily tonight.

Michael

Mother Throws A Party

Mother has decided to throw a party. This will be the first time ever that anyone has been in our apartment besides Sarah and Mrs. Lanin. I'm not sure how it all came about, but right now watching the activity that is going on is exciting. Never would I have imagined Mr. Dudley in our kitchen making Southern Fried chicken. Minnie and Selma are preparing a platter of cold cuts and vegetable boats of radishes and cucumbers. Mrs. Lanin has brought coleslaw and potato salad. In the living room, Mr. Lanin is setting out bottles of cold beer in a tub filled with ice. The Maestro and Signora are invited, too, and are bringing dessert. At the last minute I called Tommy and asked him to come, but he said he promised to take BoBo roller skating, and he can't disappoint BoBo.

"You know how that goes. Besides, you don't want me and BoBo showing up there with Lila around," said Tommy. "Not a great idea, pal, but, if we get done early, I'll drop her off and come by."

The phone rings. Mother asks me to answer it. I pick it up but I only hear the now familiar silence on the other end. The calls started right after Sarah's birthday, so I thought it was Lila, but now I'm sure it's Father. Even though he says nothing, his silence and anger about his forced exile is loud and clear. I imagine him watching the apartment house, observing the unimaginable and all he has lost. I hang up the phone. Mother comes up to me and asks, “Who was it?" I tell her it was a wrong number.

Sarah

Lila Shows Up

I just finished eating my second helping of Dudley's fried chicken and I'm stuffed. I swear I've never eaten anything so delicious. The same goes for everyone else. The platter has been picked clean. Mrs. Stein and Mom announce that desserts and coffee will be served shortly. The thought of eating anything else makes me let out a serious burp and make a run for the bathroom. I've made a pig of myself, but it was worth it, every single bite.

As I go towards the bathroom, I pass Michael's bedroom. The door is open and I walk in. I see he's been busy setting up the new bookcase and shelves that Dad and Dudley built for him. The bookcase has all of his favorite novels and a few of the new art books he's been buying. On the wall next to his bed are shelves with his sketchpads and drawing materials. I run my hands over the pads, amazed that he has so many. I pull out one of them, sit down on his bed, and flip through beautiful drawings of different scenes in the neighborhood - kids playing stickball, women shopping, parents sitting on the stoop. There's one of someone coming out of Harry's Soda Shoppe, eating an ice cream. I realize it's me. I look at the others and see that each of the scenes has someone from our block in it.

I'm so engrossed that I don't hear Michael come into the

room. "Do you like them?"

"Like them? I love them. They're wonderful! Show me!"

Michael takes two more books from the shelves and we go through them. He can draw anything - people, still-life, animals, simple flowers. He surprises me once again at how unbelievably talented he is.

Michael puts the pads away and pulls out a thick, black leather sketchbook. Inside are portraits of people we know - me of course and also strangers who have caught his interest. We go through half the book when we get to a page that has only eyes. What's fascinating and strange is that each of them seems to be looking directly at me. I want to touch them. I hesitate, afraid I might smudge something. Suddenly I feel this great need to say something really meaningful, important, about his art—something he'll never forget, but I don't have the words.

Instead, I put my hand over his and rest my head on this shoulder. "I love you, Michael."

He hugs me in the soft way that only he can. The moment is sweet. I want to stay this way forever, but fireworks suddenly erupt in my head as Lila unexpectedly sweeps into the bedroom.

"Well, aren't you two the lovebirds," she says spitefully.

Lila

Crashing The Party

Everyone here is having a good time. I can smell the food. My mouth waters at the sight of the desserts. Sure, everyone is happy to see me, or at least they pretend. They seem more curious than anything. If Hannah hadn't greeted me with her genuine smile, I probably would have walked out.

"Lila, go say hello to Sarah and Michael. They're in his room. I know they would be happy to see you," says Hannah, always so naïve.

I doubt that. Sarah is still angry at me, but it's just as well. It never would have worked anyway.

When I walk into Michael's room, the sight of the two of them sickens me. How come Sarah gets everything good in life? Even Michael, who got so badly hurt by his maniac father, has had his life turned around. And his father didn't come back. Not like my Mom did. Only I get the shit!

Michael looks surprised to see me and immediately turns to see Sarah's reaction—which is unexpected, to say the least. Well, I'm here and that's it. I know Michael's mind is going in circles right now, trying to figure out how to make this work. It's useless. I woke up this morning and decided I wanted to make someone feel bad . . . and I picked Sarah. Does she deserve it? No. But that just gives me more reason.

"Nice room, Michael. I like all the books and everything."

I walk up to the open shelves and run my finger along the sketchbooks all neatly lined up. I pull one out, thumb through it. Pretty pictures. He's good. I put the book back and turn to look at Sarah and Michael. They haven't moved an inch. On Sarah's lap is an open book. I walk over and casually take it. Sarah tries to hold on to it, but I'm stronger. I pull it away and take it with me to the open window and sit on the ledge.

As I look at each set of eyes, I'm taken back by the beauty and the honesty in each of them. The eyes are remarkable. Some of them heartbreaking. Michael sees things that I did not think possible. I wonder what he sees in mine. *Do I want to know? I'd be afraid to ask.* I continue to turn the pages. There are dozens of portraits of adults, parents, and their children, shopkeepers, teachers from school, his mother, Maestro and Signora and, of course, Sarah. There is even one of Mr. DeMarco, Tommy's father. Strange, I don't see any of Tommy. There are none of Mr. Stein, but that's no surprise.

"Wow, you have almost everyone in the South Bronx except me. How come?"

"Lila, if Michael were to draw a portrait of you, the page would go up in flames, scattering your meanness on everyone around. Now give me back that book."

Okay, now we start. Sarah tries to take the book away from me. We both tug at it till it falls to the floor. Two sheets fly out. All three of us reach for them, but I get to them first and put them behind my back. Before either of them can say anything or make a move, I hold them up in the air and wave them above my head. I stare at them and am blown away. They're both of Tommy. One is Tommy in his favorite leather jacket, looking cool and distant; the other is him from the waist up, bare-chested. I go back to the book with the eyes, find the pages. No mistake, they're Tommy's. I put it all together. These are personal. Very private.

"Ohmigod, Michael, these make Tommy look like a Greek God. I'm sure he'd love to see these." As soon as the words come out of my mouth, I'm sorry.

Michael takes the portraits and book from me. He turns away and puts them into his desk and then sits down with his back to me. At first, I feel compassion. This is why his father beat him; this is what it was all about. I wonder if Tommy knows how Michael feels about him.

I go to him, I am about to put my hand on his shoulder when Sarah plows right into me, pushing me to the floor and starts slapping my face.

"What a bitch you are! If you tell anyone about this, I will kill you," she yells.

I catch my breath and let all my unhappiness and disappointments of the last few weeks lift me up from the floor. I push Sarah onto the bed and position myself on top of her. I use one hand to hold her head and the other to cover her mouth. Michael jumps in and tries to get me off her but I kick him hard. He falls back.

"You think you're so righteous. Perfect family, friends, your lovely boy here . . . Michael, well, there are some things that stink in your life, too. Like for instance, the whole neighborhood is talking about Mrs. Stein going around with Dudley. What the hell is that all about? It's disgusting!" I say this so viciously that even I am shocked by my outburst.

But, I'm not finished, I want to hurt her even more. "And if you're thinking about running to your mother about all the things I've just said. Well, go ahead. She'll take my word over yours any day. Besides she thinks you're having some serious mental problems. She told me in secret - so there!"

None of what I just said is true. What is wrong with me? I'm a horrible person, no good, evil just like Sarah and Mom have always said.

Michael places his hands on my shoulders and pulls me off Sarah. I don't try to stop him; I've given up fighting. I look down at Sarah and then Michael. I would give anything right now to take it all back . . . but it's too late. I turn my back on the two of them and start to leave.

"Lila, before you go, you should think twice about spreading rumors and dirty lies ever again. Because, if you do, I will tell the whole world."

And then I knew. She saw us . . . it was her.

I don't ask her to take it back. I don't call her names. I just say nothing and walk out of Michael's bedroom, past Hannah, Leo, Mr. Stein, Dudley and whoever else is there. I don't belong here . . . or anywhere.

Sarah

Getting Even

Everyone is hovering over us, bombarding us with questions. There's so much tumult going on that if feels like the air is being sucked out of the room. Michael and I are sitting side by side like Siamese twins. I'm afraid to look at him. I lost it big time and maybe even Michael's friendship. I wouldn't blame him. I only wanted to protect him. But when Lila started to shoot her mouth off, saying all those horrible things . . . what was I supposed to do? *God, why can't they all leave? I need to ask Mom a question, the only one that really matters.*

Suddenly an ear-splitting whistle brings all the commotion to a halt. I look up and there's Daddy pushing everyone out the door. The only ones left are Mom and Mrs. Stein.

"Mom, may I talk to you alone, please?"

Michael faces me and with his eyes wants to know if I'm OK. I nod my head yes. He and his mother walk out of the bedroom, closing the door softly. It's just the two of us now. I feel sick to my stomach, but, if I don't ask the question now, I never will.

"Do you love Lila more than me?" I ask Mom, almost choking on my words.

Mom stares at me with such hopelessness that I expect her

to throw her arms around me and swear it isn't true, but she doesn't do that.

"Sarah, I love you more than life. You are my miracle. That you can ask me this is more hurtful than I can say. I don't know what happened here but this foolishness with Lila can't go on like this. I'm not sure what to do, but something has to be done."

I don't know what I expected her to say, but her declaration of love doesn't convince me. The realization that Lila may be right, that Mom is tired of me and that she may think I'm crazy, hits home. Before she can say another word, I bolt out the door.

Daddy and Mom are calling after me to come back, I can't. *But where can I go? Right now even Tar Beach doesn't feel like a safe haven for me.* I head for the street.

When I get tired of walking around the neighborhood, I start for home. It's late. Mom and Dad will be waiting for me in the kitchen, asking for an explanation or . . . maybe they will just rush to take me in their arms and say how sorry they are, but for what? It's all me; I'm the one who should say I'm sorry. I was wrong. Lila is full of lies and I let her get to me. After what I saw in the park she can be capable of anything.

To my surprise there is no one waiting up for me. On the table is a plate with some cookies and a note. *Tomorrow we talk. I love you.* Just as well . . . I'm so tired and still have too much to think about.

It's impossible to go to sleep - too much going around in my head, images of Lila and Max in each other's arms, Mom staring at me as if I'm something she wants to get rid of. I know I'm being paranoid; everything is twisted, and my brain can't take it all in. Sitting up in bed, I turn on the light and pick up a movie magazine on my night table. In the centerfold is a spread on a new movie starring Natalie Wood and Gene Kelly called *Marjorie Morningstar*. The story is about a young girl who falls in love with an older man. Everyone is talking about it - it's supposed to be very daring. Not like *Lolita*, of course. That was different. No, this is about true love. The photo shows the two of them gazing into each other's eyes, their arms around each other. I linger over the page and tear it out from the magazine. I keep staring at the photo.

An idea comes to me.

I open the drawer to my desk, take out a pair of scissors, an envelope, and a box of crayons. With yellow and ochre crayons I carefully color over Natalie Wood's dark hair. Admiring my work, I decide to go one step further. In a childlike scrawl, I write the names Lila and Max over the heads of Natalie Wood and Gene Kelly. Now there is no stopping me. I don't think, just act. I fold the picture and put into an envelope, sealing it with my lips. I sneak out of the apartment in bare feet and run to the Rosens' door.

Suddenly I'm not so sure. If I do this, there is no turning back. I start to sweat and step back from the door. I should walk away, go home, but then Lila's words bounce back into my head. I see the image of Mom looking at me the way she did.

I slip the envelope underneath the door.

June - July

Hannah

Sounds of menacing footsteps and hushed voices, feelings of confusion and fear so thick you can't find your way out. I try to find my parents, brother, and sister. I can hear them shouting out for me. Then I hear the thud of soldiers' boots, then the shots!

"Hannah, wake up, you're safe. You're not in the camps, you're here with me and Sarah, and it's all right. You're just dreaming again," Leo says out loud, trying to comfort me.

He is used to my nightmares; we both have them, but his have been put away for a time now. Mine still haunt me. I open my eyes and take in my surroundings. It always takes a while for my heart to settle down. Leo holds me till I stop shaking. But I still hear noises . . . someone is pounding on our door. Quickly he lets go of me. He puts on his pants and shoes and goes into the living room. I hear him open the front door, and walk out into the hallway. He's gone only a few seconds when he runs back into the bedroom and tells me to get dressed. Something has happened at the Rosens'. Sarah is already in the living room. Looking scared, she wants to go with us, but Leo tells her to stay put and lock the door.

I walk out in the hallway and see everyone from our floor standing together in a group, tightly locked together, pointing and staring at the door to the Rosens' apartment. They're all in their pajamas or robes. I ask Leo, "What time is it?" He shows me his watch. It's four in the morning. Whatever made everyone leave their beds to congregate together in this hallway is over. The silence coming from inside the apartment makes everyone step back. Leo tries the door but it's locked. Softly, I put my head to the door and call out "Fritzy," then "Max," then "Lila." No one answers.

Leo is about to try again when there is a click. The door slowly opens. Fritzy is standing in a faded nightgown stained with perspiration and tears. Her all too familiar red blotches cover her face. Her eyes are swollen and almost closed - she looks like a mad woman. "Disgusting animals they are!"

Fritzy steps aside as Leo and I walk in. I close the door behind me. I don't know where to look first; it's as if a hurricane has gone through here. Tables and lamps are overturned. There are scattered Polaroid photos all over the floor, most of them torn to shreds. But some pieces are large enough to recognize who is in the photos. I bend down and brush my hands over them. I see her eyes, lips, hands, mouth and her blond hair. All of them are of Lila. My stomach turns. I look up; there is Max sitting in a chair, his head in his hands, whimpering like a baby.

"Max, where is she?" I scream.

Fritzy growls something and points to the bedroom.

"She's a witch you know. She made him do this. I had to beat her to get the devil out!" Fritzy yells.

In the corner of her room, Lila is crouched like a cat ready to attack. Her baby doll nightgown is ripped; there are red welts on her arms and legs. When I kneel down to hold her, she flinches in pain. Her back has been hit with a belt. I put my hand on her shoulder she immediately raises her hands over her head.

"No more. Please, no more," Lila moans.

I take a blanket off the bed and gently place it over her shoulders. Taking care not to hurt her, I lift her up from the floor as carefully as I can. Leo walks in, sees Lila, and has to turn his face away. Seeing the shock on his face, makes me realize that no one else should see Lila like this. She has been through enough.

"Leo, clear the hallway and make sure they all go back to their apartments. Take Fritzy to Minnie and Selma's. When you finish with that, come back here and we will take Lila home with us. Then you will have to go back to the Rosens' apartment and put everything in order ... and Leo, pick up everything from the floor and throw it in a garbage bag and bring it home with you."

When he is done with the neighbors and Fritzy, Leo comes back. He lifts Lila up in his arms and carries her out of the bedroom. Lila keeps her eyes closed as we walk through the living room. Before I close the door, I turn to take another look at all the bits and pieces of photos that look like a bizarre picture puzzle of Lila's face. As I turn to leave, something else catches my eye. I bend down and pick up a torn page from a magazine; it's a picture of two movie stars kissing. I look closer; someone colored over them and wrote Lila and Max's name on it. The crude drawing upsets me so much that I bite down on my lip hard enough to taste blood. I pick it up, put it in my pocket, and leave.

When we get home, Sarah is waiting for us. As she looks at Lila, she knows this is not the time to ask any questions. She helps me put Lila on my bed. As soon as I am sure Lila is asleep, I take Sarah in my arms.

"Sarah, I will never let anyone hurt you, ever!"

Leo walks in later. His face is white as a ghost.

"Hannah, he's gone."

"What do you mean 'gone'?" I ask.

"Like I said, he's gone! The bastard left. I could kill him, Hannah, I mean it."

Leo hands me the garbage bag with the photos and I put them in our bedroom closet. That night, Leo slept on the couch. In the morning, I found Sarah asleep outside our bedroom door.

Lila has been here now for a few weeks. After the first night, Sarah insisted that Lila sleep in her room, in her bed. Sarah slept on the couch. But when I went to check on them each night, I always found Sarah in her room, wrapped in a blanket and sleeping on the floor as Lila cried in her sleep.

Lila still has not spoken. When she is up, I bathe her, and change her clothes, Sarah tenderly brushes Lila's beautiful blond hair. Dr. Marx has come to look at Lila. He says that only rest will help now and after that, who knows. When I see the emptiness in Lila's eyes, I wonder if she will ever be able to forget. After all, she is just a child.

I am also worrying about my Sarah. I let her stay home the first week Lila was here but then sent her back to school. Twice, I have been called by her teacher to come and pick her up because she wasn't feeling well. She is not eating and she looks pale. I have to do something. Tonight, after Sarah helps feed Lila, I tell her that Dad is going to stay with Lila while we go out. She starts to argue with me but I say we are not going far, just to Tar Beach. Minnie and Selma helped set up everything. When we open the door and step out on Tar Beach, we are taken aback by how beautiful the evening is - the sky is filled with stars. A table is set with lit candles, a platter of mini sandwiches, and a lazy Susan with all of Sarah's favorite desserts. She smiles for the first time in weeks. We spend the time talking about little things, then about her going to Performing Arts in the fall.

"Mom, do you think Lila will be going to school with me?"

Before I can answer her, Sarah's emotions erupt and she tells me everything that happened that night - her anger at Lila threatening to expose Michael's drawings of Tommy, Lila's malicious words about her and Mrs. Stein and Dudley, words that were sharp as knives. Then Sarah described what she had seen in the park. Watching Lila and Max, what they were doing, and how wrong it seemed. She couldn't understand it, and even felt sorry for Lila, but it was the horrible accusations about me, her mother that hurt the most.

Then she told me about the magazine photo and what she had done.

"I'm so sorry. Everything is my fault. Will she ever be able to forgive me?"

I look at my only child and know that there are not enough words to make her feel better, that, being who she is, she will live with this for a long, long time. All I can do for her now is to tell her that I love her.

At the end of the evening, I ask Sarah if she would like to

sleep with me and Dad in our bed. Sarah falls into my arms and says “yes”.

For the first time in weeks, the three of us sleep through the night. I get up and announce I am making breakfast. Sarah jumps out of bed and says she will help, but, first, she's going to check on Lila. It's a matter of seconds before I hear Sarah crying out. Leo and I run into her bedroom where Sarah is standing against the wall, a look of fright and surprise on her face. The bed has been perfectly made up. Sarah points to the bed; on top, there is a note. Leo picks it up and gives it to me to read.

“Dear Hannah, Leo, and Sarah, thank you for the only kindness I have ever had.”

Leo walks out right away. He picks up the phone and calls Fritzy.

"Is she there?" He asks. "Is she with you?"

Sarah and I are standing next to him when he looks at the phone with disgust.

"She said ‘no’ and hung up."

Everyone from the neighborhood helped look for Lila. Dudley drove all around the South Bronx, searching the streets. It didn't take long to figure out that Max was gone, too. By the end of the day, both were nowhere to be found. We called the police. They questioned Fritzy for days. From that point on, her door was closed to everyone. Around the first week in June, an officer came by to tell us that there was no trace of Lila or . . . Max. "Maybe one day they'll turn up," he said.

Each night for the next few weeks people sat outside on their chairs, playing cards, and gossiping. The big news of the day was about Adolf Eichmann, an organizer of the Holocaust, being captured and charged for war crimes in Israel. Normally for us survivors that's all we would have been talking about, but it was Lila and Max's disappearance that filled our minds every day. The rumors about them were out of control. They mushroomed in size every day. Everyone had their own ideas, and suspicions - from Max taking Lila to Hollywood to become a movie star, to taking her to Israel to live with cousins, to the two of them joining a circus. When, I heard that last one, I decided to stop coming downstairs. I refused to listen to any more nonsense. I told Leo and Sarah to do the same.

Then one early summer evening at the end of July, while the usual conversations about Lila and Max were going on, Minnie and Selma, who were stationed at their window, looking out on the street, started to shout. They were so excited and rattled that is was hard to understand them. But, when they began to point, everyone stood up and gaped as they watched Max Rosen walk down the block. He looked frail and helpless. When he got to the building, each person automatically stepped aside to let him through as he struggled to climb the steps. No one said a word.

From that night on, Max hid in his apartment, except for the few times that Fritzy took him out for a walk, always holding him by the hand as if he were a small boy. Some people swore that they had never seen her look so happy. And why not? After all, for the first time, Fritzy had Max all to herself.

August

Sarah

Last Journal Entry

Well, I've done it. I've written my very last entry. You are now the bearer of all my secrets, fears, nightmares, fantasies and desires. I know it sounds all pretty dramatic, but it's true. The question is what do I do with you now?

Do I toss you in the garbage bag, never to be found again, or do I take you with me to my new bedroom in our new apartment on the other side of the Bronx, as a reminder of when Lila and I were kids: a reminder of all the games that we played, of all of the things that she did to me and made me do to her, making me feel dirty and evil. Do I want to remember how sick I felt when I saw Lila and Max kissing, reminding me of Humbert Humbert and *Lolita*, or how quick she was to hurt Michael by threatening to expose his drawings to Tommy? But, worst of all was her threat to spread ugly rumors about Mom, the one person who truly cared for her, just to spite me. When Mom had brought her home and I saw the bruises and welts from Fritzy's beating, I could hardly hold my tears back, but I knew if I didn’t I wouldn't be able to stop.

If I hadn't altered that magazine picture, maybe Fritzy would never have found the Polaroids, Lila wouldn't have been beaten, and she and Max wouldn't have disappeared. I hope Max did something good for Lila and found her a safe place to live. Maybe his coming back alone and giving himself to Fritzy as her prisoner was his punishment. Mom has tried to comfort me by repeating over and over that, even though what I did was wrong, I was not to blame.

"After seeing those pictures, I knew something bad was going to happen," she said.

But it doesn't matter to me anymore because I don't want to remember - I want to forget, to be free of it all, free of Lila.

And then my wish came true. A few weeks after Max came back, Mom and Dad told me that we were moving. There was too much sadness around us. We needed a fresh start.

"It will be good for all of us," Mom said, holding back her emotions.

So here we are, ready to go. The car is packed. Dad and Dudley are waiting.

Michael and his mother are downstairs to say goodbye, although this goodbye doesn't count. In a week they also will be moving just a few blocks from us. Michael holds me tight; we all hug and part. Dudley starts the car and begins to slowly drive away. Dad sits up front with him; Mom is with me in the back seat. I turn around and look out the back window. Mom takes my hand. I stretch my neck to see if Fritzy or Max is at the window, but the shade is down. I close my eyes and pretend Lila is standing there, waving good-bye.

Epilogue

1980

Max Rosen knocked softly on his daughter's apartment door on the Upper West Side. After a few seconds and no response, he knocked louder, then he used the key he had been given by Lila (to be used only in emergencies) and let himself in. Normally he would have waited a bit longer but he was late; traffic had held him up and he needed to get Lila to the airport. She was once again going off to London and then on to Japan for business. What kind of business he never really knew. He had been told by Lila a long time ago not to ask questions.

When he entered the designer-decorated apartment, he called out her name, and looked around. Although there was nothing out of order and her suitcase was at the door, ready to go, he knew immediately that something was wrong. He stood in the center of the living room and again called his daughter's name. No answer. Max turned his head and gazed at the slightly open door to Lila's bedroom. Fear gripped his heart and a cold sweat drenched his entire body. Barely able to breathe, he swung the door open and released a roar of anguish great enough to break anyone's heart and soul forever. Max Rosen found his daughter lying on her bed, her silk robe slightly open, her hands carefully arranged, one behind her head, one at her side. Her shoulder-length golden blonde hair had been artistically placed on the mound of delicate, blood stained lace pillows. Except for the stone cold eyes staring at him and the sharp red lines around her neck, Lila looked like the movie star she had always dreamt of becoming. Whoever killed her must have loved and hated her at the same time. For Max, the love of his life, his reason for living was . . . dead.

A well-known drug dealer, who was also Lila's lover, was brought in for questioning. He was held without bail for the murder of Lila Rosen. The newspapers had a field day. Photographs were shown of Lila in various trend-setting places all over Europe and Israel. The trial went on for several weeks. Max Rosen attended the trial every day. But, because of insufficient evidence and an air-tight alibi, there was no conviction.

Six months after the trial, Sarah landed the role of Karen Wright, one of the two lead roles in the revival of *The Children's Hour*. When she had gotten the news, her first thought was, wouldn't it have been something if Lila played Martha Dobie, the other lead? She laughed and then wept.

About The Author

Rose Ross is the only child of Holocaust survivors. The stories of her parents, other survivors, and the second generation children she grew up with was the motivation for her novel, *LILA*. She lives in Delray Beach, Florida.

Acknowledgements

I thank my first writing group, who made me believe in myself and help me find my voice - Cecele Krauss, Mary Gail Biebel, Gwen Gould, Karen Jahn, who is no longer with us but whom I think about often, my editor Barbara Cronie, editor of Par Excellence and program director of The Writers Colony at Old School Square in Delray Beach, Florida, where my book first emerged. My readers, Tom Orgazont, Hazel Lada, Bobbi Kotler, Kim Goodyear, Carolyn Schroth, Wendy Levitt, Susan Vazquez, Deb Pines, Joyce Prigot. Special thanks to Tina Springer-Miller, Kristen Murtaugh, and my children Ed and Sarah. I am especially grateful to Maria Nhambu, who lifted me up when I needed it and to Patricia Shuman, who was always there for me when I felt lost, and a very heartfelt thank you to Mort Butler who with her indomitable patience made my book a reality.

Made in the USA
Middletown, DE
02 April 2021

36761244R00142